Kidnapped JUSTICE

....
THE 4TH BOOK OF THE
ARKANSAS OIL DAYS SERIES

KUDU

BRENDA HUTCHESON FICKEY

Kidnapped Justice

by Brenda Hutcheson Fickey

Trade paperback ISBN: 9781938624339
Ebook ISBN: 9781938624346

Cover design by Martijn van Tilborgh

Kidnapped Justice is also available on Amazon Kindle, Barnes & Noble Nook and Apple iBooks.

For more information and to purchase more books by Brenda Fickey, visit *BrendaFickey.com.*

Contents

Dedication

for the Hutcheson great-grandchildren—
Kyle, Beth, Keremy, Ethan,
Timmy, Michael, Sydney, Olivia,
Josh, Dax, Kannyn, Emma, and Matthew

Acknowledgements

It is with great pleasure I express my thanks to those who have helped me move my ideas to the printed pages called Kidnapped Justice. I want to thank Kudu Publishing (Martijn, Dave, and Matt) for catching the vision for my stories. It is a privilege to partner with you. Your ideas have breathed life into my work in ways I could never have realized without your help. A very special thank you goes to Tommie and the Smackover Chamber of Commerce for the use of information and ideas from the private ghost walk my sister and I took during the midnight hour to get a feel for the town in 1925. There is so much more to come from that tour in future books. I thank my editing team (Olivia, Joni, and Leslie) for the numerous readings they did and the suggestions they made to make sure the storyline was credible and consistent with past plots. Another part of their job was to make sure my scenes flowed well together and created an exciting read for fans and future readers. The success of Kidnapped Justice is as much yours as it is mine. Thank you, Dad, for keeping an eye out for newspaper articles and other pertinent information to help with the historical features of my stories and the authenticity of the region. I also want to thank my fans, both those I have had since I began writing The Arkansas Oil Days Collection and the new ones I have added with this book. It is a pleasure to write for you.

Chapter 1

Hank opened his eyes and blinked several times before closing them again, too sleepy to be curious about what woke him this time. *Go back to sleep. It'll be time to get up for school soon enough.* He turned toward the wall and pulled the covers up to his chin, snuggling against the chill of the late September night.

"Wake up, Hank."

In one fluid motion, he opened his eyes, sat up, and folded the covers back, the chill in the room waking his senses.

"Okay, I'm up."

He rubbed the sleep from his eyes with his palms, yawned, and sat on the edge of the bed. Out of habit, he looked out the window. He stared at the stars and the crescent-shaped moon. *Huh? What time is it? Whoa, better question, who woke me?* Then he heard something bump against the outside wall just below the open bedroom window. *That coon must be trying to get in for the third time this week.* He sat still, listening. A dog barked in the distance, then he heard voices. The hair on his neck and arms bristled. *That's not a coon. That's whispering...at least two people arguing.* He scrunched his brows together. *What in the world?* He got on his hands and knees.

Be strong and courageous.

Startled, he sat on his haunches as his brain registered the voice in his head.

"Wha…?" He glanced around the room, then out the window. "That didn't come from outside, but who…" He didn't realize he'd spoken out loud.

The sound of pounding feet moving away from the house drew his attention back to the window. He shivered as he scrambled off the bed. When his feet touched the cold floor, his toes curled. In the rush to get to the window, his little toe caught the corner of the bedpost.

"Ouch." He grabbed his foot and hopped in place. *Sh-h-h! Are you trying to wake up Jimmy?*

He froze in a one-legged stance as his heart skipped a couple of beats and stared at his nine-year-old brother's empty bed. As Hank stood on both feet, his stubbed toe forgotten, terror gripped his heart with sharp claws. He grasped the footboard for support, and then swallowed past a thick lump in his throat. *Where's Jimmy Jack?* Every nerve tingled from his scalp to the bottoms of his feet. He focused on the scene outside the window. Movement among the shadows, cast by the moon's waning glow, caught his attention.

All else forgotten, he ran to the window. When he leaned out as far as he could without falling, he saw three shadowy figures in the yard. A light breeze added to the chill washing over him. Apprehension triggered violent shudders throughout his body. He bumped his head on the windowsill.

"Hey, stop! Where's my brother?"

He watched as the trespassers hid behind the thick trunk of the sweet gum tree in the driveway before they ran toward the woods. One had something slung over his shoulder like a large sack of potatoes. Hank could only take shallow breaths. In a panic, he climbed out the window without getting shoes or changing out of his pajamas.

The three prowlers blended into the woods as they took the trail Hank used to get to his fishing hole near the Ouachita River. Before he knew what was happening, he sprinted across the yard between the house and the edge of the Baker property. A dreadful sense of foreboding stopped him at the trailhead. His chest heaved with every breath. His heart and lungs hurt, and tears streamed down his face. He squeezed his eyes shut and collapsed to his knees, hugging his shaking body. *I need to think.* Thin wisps of vapor escaped from his chattering teeth.

A vision flashed across his memory of a cabin deep in the woods between Cross Roads and Peanut Hill. It belonged to the bootleggers who had kidnapped him three months ago. Anger replaced his fear and crept into the core of his being until a dam of rage burst, flooding his soul. He put his hands on his knees as he sat back on his heels. Then he shook his fists at God, gazing into the depths of the dark heavens overhead. His prayer echoed off the trees.

"Who was I chasing just now? Where's my brother? Haven't you caused me enough pain this summer? What do you want from me?"

Trust your heart and not your eyes, Hank. Act wisely because there will be times you'll need to trust your eyes and not your heart.

He stood as heat spread up from his neck to his cheeks. Rigid, clenched fists pounded his thighs. "What..."

Someone touched his shoulder. He spun around so fast dizziness knocked him to the ground.

"Hank, honey, what's the matter with you? You're going to be late for school."

The scenery had changed from the woods to his bedroom, and he raised himself on shaky elbows. His head ached behind his furrowed brows. *That was just a dream? It was so real.* He wiped moisture from around his ears with his forearm and looked over at his brother's empty bed, neatly made.

His heart skipped a beat. "Where's Jimmy Jack?"

"He's eating breakfast. Son, you're very pale." Ma sat beside him and put a warm hand on his shoulders. "And you're trembling. Are you feeling okay?"

"Yeah, Ma, I'm fine...really. Sorry I overslept." He hugged her, almost afraid to let go. Finally, he sat up and braced his hands on his knees, locking his elbows to keep them steady. His mind searched for an explanation for the dream. "Uh, I'll get dressed fast so I'll have time to eat."

"If you're sure you're okay." She patted his hands and stood to leave. "I'll keep your food warm." He smiled until she shut the door. Then he blew out a long, solemn sigh.

Hank flopped back onto his pillow. *That's the most disturbing dream I've had in a while.* He sat up on his elbows again. *I hope it's not another one of* those *dreams.* His stomach rumbled as the smell of bacon, coffee, biscuits, and fried eggs filtered through his thoughts. He rolled out of bed and dressed, straightening up before leaving.

As he made his way to the kitchen, he heard the familiar voice of Deputy Pete Collins. It had taken a while for Hank to enjoy the deputy coming around all the time. What really impressed him now was how much like his late daddy Mr. Pete was. It was like having Daddy home again...almost.

When he sat at the table, his stomach growled.

"Hurry up and eat your breakfast, honey. Pete is taking you boys to school this morning."

How does she do that? Without looking, she knows when I'm in the room. He took a sip of milk and watched the deputy wipe the table. Then he tossed the cloth into the pan Ma kept in the sink for washing dishes.

The deputy put an arm around Ma's shoulders. "Boys, your ma and I have an announcement to make, and we wanted you two to be the first to hear it." Hank noticed the smile on her face and the glow in her eyes as she looked up at him. "I asked your ma to marry me last night, and she said yes."

Jimmy yelped like an Indian. Hank smiled and nodded as joy, with a hint of sadness, warmed his heart. As he gulped down the rest of his milk, the fear and uncertainty of the dream and its meaning diminished.

Mr. Pete chuckled. "We're thinking about Sunday, the first of November before the potluck, since everyone we'd invite to the wedding will already be at the church. We still need to finalize things with Pastor Bob, but what do you think?"

"It's about time." Jimmy Jack jumped from his chair and gave the man a bear hug around his waist. "What took you so long to ask her?"

Tears threatened to flow from Hank's eyes as his grin widened till his cheeks ached. *That's Daddy's birthday.* Then, with blatant clarity, the events from the dream ambushed the celebration.

Trust your heart and not your eyes, Hank. Act wisely because there will be times you'll need to trust your eyes and not your heart.

The anger he had expressed toward God in his dream took root in Hank's heart.

* * * * * * *

The excitement about the wedding could not dispel the uneasiness of the dream. Both kept Hank from concentrating on his lessons all morning. He was glad when Daniel and Beth Ann joined him for lunch. Every day, they ate under the sweet gum tree at the edge of the Cross Roads school property. Because it was so close to the woods surrounding the schoolyard, it was the best place to talk freely, away from the rest of the kids.

The friendship the three shared kept Hank from losing hope when his daddy was declared missing in action in 1918, after the Battle of Belleau Wood in France, near the end of the war. When his body was found and his bones were buried this summer, seven years later, Daniel and Beth Ann stayed close to Hank and cried with him after the funeral till he felt better. It was uncanny how they read each others' minds.

Daniel tossed his apple core over the fence. "You're awful quiet, Hank. Is everything all right at home?"

Beth Ann looked in his lunch pail. "You didn't eat your lunch. Don't you feel well?"

The scowl on her face reminded him of her daddy. Dr. Warden had the same look when he examined Hank back in June. He had a bump on the back of his head from being knocked unconscious by his kidnappers. "I'm fine, just thinking about stuff."

"You look like someone gave you a black eye, or are you just having trouble sleeping?" Worry lines creased her forehead.

"Everything's fine." Hank decided to wait to tell them about the wedding. He was too preoccupied with the voice. If it really was just a dream, then why did the voice tell him the exact same thing when he was wide awake? "I'm not sick, and I'm not having any trouble sleeping—not yet anyway. I've just got a lot on my..."

Daniel hiccupped then burped. He put his hand on his chest and sniffed. "Excuse me. Oh, boy, does that hurt. I hate doing that." He hiccupped again. "Sorry, you were saying?" After a couple more hiccups, he took a deep breath and held it till his face turned red.

Hank chuckled. He felt the tension from the morning release itself as a sense of normalcy took its place. "I had a dream this morning, and I can't get it out of my head for some reason."

Daniel slowly let the breath out of his puffy cheeks. "Uh, oh. How many times have you had this one?"

"I was going to ask the same thing." Beth Ann divided the fried apple pie from her lunch in two, giving a piece to Hank after Daniel passed on the offer. She licked the filling from her fingers. "We've come to expect your dreams to be more than they seem, especially after this summer. I know you don't like them, but you do seem to have a special gift where they're concerned."

Hank cradled the pie with both hands, savoring the smell of apples, sugar, and cinnamon. "Thanks." He put the whole piece into his mouth and thought about their comments while he chewed.

After he swallowed, he licked each finger clean. "I'm not sure I want this one to be one of those kinds of dreams. I've only had it once, but it's bothering me more than the others for some reason."

A bell clanged, startling them.

Hank looked at his uneaten food, suddenly hungry. "I can't believe lunch is over already."

They gathered their pails and ambled toward the others going inside.

Beth Ann stopped, wiping dirt from her backside. "Hey, isn't that the sheriff with Miss Taylor?"

They all watched as the teacher with the bell looked around the schoolyard then gazed in their direction.

"I wonder why he's here." Daniel looked behind them. "Huh, she's pointing at us."

Every nerve in Hank's face itched as he watched the sheriff walk toward them. "No, she's pointing at me." His knees threatened to give out as the man made eye contact with him.

Beth Ann balanced herself with a hand around Hank's upper arm while she took a rock out of her shoe. "From the look on his face, I'd say it's serious, whatever it is."

"Yeah, you'd better go on back to class. We'll talk later. Let's meet at my house after school, and then we'll go to the fishing hole." His pulse beat harder with every step the man took, closing the distance between them. His friends walked past the sheriff, and then looked back at him a couple of times before getting in line.

"I've come to take you home, son. The principal knows you're leaving for the rest of the day, so go on and get your things. Your ma's waiting for us."

"What's wrong, sheriff?" He shivered before he felt the warmth of the man's hand on his shoulder as they walked back to the school building. The dream flashed through Hank's mind. His pulse quickened as he searched the faces of the students in line. "Is Jimmy okay?"

Chapter 2

"There's been a development and a situation I need to share with you and your ma. Don't you worry about your brother; he's fine. Pete's meeting us at your house, and then he'll pick Jimmy Jack up after school." He held the door open for Hank. "Get your things, now, and let's not make them wait too long at home."

"Yes sir." Hank heard the door close just before he spotted his teacher in the hallway outside his classroom. She smiled as she held up his books, but the look on her face reminded him of Ma when she worried.

"I hope everything's all right, hon. Take care, and I'll see you Monday morning."

Everything moved in slow motion as he took his things. "Yes, ma'am, thank you, Miss Martin." The hallway stretched before him as he located the sheriff outside the principal's office. He was glad he hadn't eaten anything other than part of Beth Ann's fried pie. He felt pressure under his chin and the familiar tingle from his jaw line to behind his ears as nausea churned in his stomach.

The door squeaked as the sheriff opened it. "Come on, son. We need to get going."

The quiet, bumpy ride home seemed to take forever. When they finally turned into the driveway, Hank watched Ma and Mr. Pete get up from the porch swing, holding hands. His heart hammered so hard in his chest he was sure the sheriff could hear it. Once they were all inside, the adults took their seats, Ma and Mr. Pete on the divan and the sheriff in one of the chairs across the room from them.

"Oh, dear, I'm a terrible hostess. Would you like some coffee, Stan?"

"No, ma'am, I'm fine."

Hank's pulse quickened as he set his books on the hearth, every nerve jittery. He sat in the chair closest to the fireplace, clasping his hands in his lap and hoping to get warm. Dread gnawed at his gut; a shiver shook his spine.

"Before we begin, I understand congratulations are in order."

"Yes, thank you, but we can talk about that later. Right now, I'm more than a little nervous. What's happened, and why is it necessary for my son to be here?"

Hank tried to breathe deeply. He feared he would hyperventilate.

"Yes, ma'am, I'm sorry. I'll get right to the point. As you know, the man who kidnapped Hank this past June is about to go to trial. However, due to today's events, his trial has been postponed indefinitely. Al Higgins has escaped from jail along with at least a couple of others, and the concern is he's coming here."

The dream…it's…

"Neither Pete nor I think Hank is in any real danger, but we wanted you to know just in case he shows up. And we wanted you to hear it from us first."

Hank sucked air into his lungs so fast he choked on his spit. The more he tried to suppress the coughing fit, the worse the tickle in his throat became. Finally, he buried his mouth in the crook of his arm just as the coughing began in earnest. Heat spread up from his chest to his face. He stood and faced the mantle as he pressed his fists against his throbbing temples. The cough persisted with a vengeance.

A hand pressed against his back between his shoulder blades.

"Are you all right, son?"

He jumped as he spun to face Mr. Pete, his eyes wide open.

"Whoa! Take it easy. I didn't mean to scare you."

Hank saw the deep worry lines on the deputy's forehead and continued to cough into his fist, still unable to catch his breath or speak. He waved the deputy back to his seat with his other hand and sat back down. Sweat beaded on his upper lip and forehead.

"I'm sorry. I'll be fine." His raspy voice scratched his throat; the tickle started a new wave of coughs. He wiped the tears from his eyes as his coughing subsided. Mr. Pete sat beside him and gently patted between his shoulder blades.

"Here, take this. Are you okay, now?"

He took the handkerchief from the deputy and blew his nose. "Yes sir. I just need something to drink."

"Sit here; I'll get it."

When Mr. Pete returned to the hearth and gave him the glass of water, everyone settled again and focused on the sheriff. The older man and long-time Baker family friend bowed his head, and then took a deep breath and let it out slowly. "Well, I'm afraid there's more we need to tell you."

Uncle Will.

That voice again... "It's about Uncle Will, isn't it?"

"Will?" The pain in Ma's voice pierced Hank's heart. The deputy joined her on the divan, again.

"Yes, ma'am, it's about Will. Just after we got the news about the escape, we got a call from the warden at the penitentiary."

She raised the fist holding her handkerchief to her cheek. "Did he escape, too?"

"No, ma'am, he's in the infirmary."

Tears formed in Hank's eyes and fear threatened to choke him. The nausea returned. *The dream! God, please don't let Uncle Will be dead...please!* He was surprised at the spontaneous prayer.

"According to the report we received, he was attacked in the rock yard. One of the other convicts stabbed him several times, and cut his face pretty badly. Another convict who witnessed the attack identified your brother, but he won't name the attacker." Ma sobbed. "I'm very sorry to have to tell you this news, ma'am. At least he's alive...for now, but he's in really bad shape."

"Oh, praise God!" Ma whimpered as Hank silently thanked the Lord, too.

"The doctor will know in a couple of days if he'll make it, and if he does, he isn't sure about how his face will heal."

"I understand."

"As things develop with his recovery they'll let us know, and then we'll let you know. For now, there's nothing else to do but wait and see."

Hank scanned the room. The scene before him seemed unreal, more like a moving picture show. He observed Mr. Pete hold Ma as she sobbed against his chest. He watched the sheriff sit back after getting a handkerchief from his back pants pocket and wiping his eyes and mouth with it.

Sheriff Stan cleared his throat. "Did you know Will had visits with Pinkerton detectives and an agent from the William J. Burns Detective Agency?"

Ma sat up, shaking her head. "No. Why would they be interested in my brother?"

"He had asked to meet with them. According to reports made to the warden, Will was set to testify against Higgins."

"Is that why he was attacked?"

"That's one possibility they're looking into." The sheriff blew his nose.

The deputy pulled an envelope from his uniform shirt pocket and handed it to Ma.

"This is for you from Will, but it was addressed to our office. Please understand; the warden reads all the mail that goes out and comes in at the prison, for the safety of all concerned. That's the only reason it's been opened already. He wants you to know they're doing everything they can to find out what happened. If there's anything Stan or I can do, we will. Just let us know, okay?"

She nodded and stared at the envelope for several seconds before taking it in shaky hands. "I don't know what to say except…thank you. Thank you both."

In the quiet of the moment, Hank relived the afternoon he was kidnapped while he walked home from the fishing hole. He sucked in another quick breath and made eye contact with Mr. Pete, panic squeezing his chest.

"What is it, son?"

"There was another man with Uncle Will and Mr. Higgins… uh…Harry."

"That's right, Stan. He was the quiet one in the cabin. I think his name is Sawyer, Harold Sawyer, no middle name."

"Uncle Will was more afraid of Mr. Higgins, sheriff, but he was afraid of Mr. Sawyer, too."

Ma looked between the sheriff and Mr. Pete. "Did he escape with this Higgins?"

The sheriff jotted the information in a small notebook before replacing it in his shirt pocket. "We should have the list of names by the time we get back to the office. I'll check it and let you know. In the meantime, keep a lookout for both of them, you hear? You remember what they look like, don't you, son?"

"Yes sir, I won't ever forget their faces."

The sheriff stood and put his handkerchief back in his pants pocket. "Well, if there's nothing else, we'd best get back to the office, Pete, and finish things up before you're off duty tonight.

Martha, I don't think any of you have anything to worry about immediately; but Hank, you make sure you and your brother let your ma know where you are at all times, son. You folks have a good rest of the day and weekend, ma'am." He hiked his pants, and then walked to the door.

The deputy stood, but hesitated to leave with the sheriff. "Give me a minute, Stan?"

"Sure." The older man shut the door quietly behind him, and then his footfalls on the porch faded.

Mr. Pete took Ma's hands in his and kissed them. "I don't want you to worry about a thing, either of you." He glanced at Hank then back at Ma. "We're on the lookout for Higgins, just in case he does come around here. If you see or hear anything suspicious, let me know right away." The deputy hugged Ma before grabbing his hat from the lamp table beside the divan. "We're also waiting for return calls from the detective agencies, so we can learn as much about their visits as possible. We hope to hear back from them later today. I'll let you know what we find out." He took a few steps toward the door then stopped and turned toward Hank. "I'll make you a promise, son. I won't let anything happen to you, your ma, or Jimmy Jack. You believe that, don't you?"

"Yes sir."

"I need to go, now." Deputy Collins opened the door. "Try not to worry. I'll be back with Jimmy when school's out."

* * * * * * *

Hank loved going to Catfish Haven. He could still remember the day his daddy told him about *his* first time here with Grandpa. It's the biggest Baker family secret in Frenchport and the best fishing hole on the Ouachita River. The news the sheriff had delivered set Hank on edge. He figured catching one or two of the five-plus pound bottom-feeders would calm his nerves because they fought the hardest. He needed the distraction to clear his mind of the looming situation engulfing him. As soon as Daniel and

Beth Ann arrived after school they set off for a couple of hours of fishing before evening chores and supper.

Daniel stepped in front of the other two and walked backwards as they made their way across the open field to the trail in the woods. "Hey, we're still going to Smackover tomorrow, aren't we? You, me, Deputy Collins, and Abraham are picking up supplies for your ma and Granny, right?"

Beth Ann chuckled. "Now, there's a surprise I didn't see coming. I never would have thought it possible. Daniel Wagner is actually excited about helping Granny Rose. How'd you manage that, Hank?"

A smile spread across his face. "I'm not sure what happened. Maybe he's just getting used to her. You know, the more he's around her, the less scared of her he is."

"I never said I was scared of her. I'm aware. Doesn't the Bible say something about not tempting God? Let's just say, I'm cautiously optimistic about having a healthy respect for her."

Hank rolled his eyes and looked at Beth Ann. Both grinned and shook their heads. Daniel shrugged his shoulders and fell in line with them, putting Beth Ann between himself and Hank.

"Besides, I miss Abraham now that school's started. I got used to him being with us most every day."

Beth Ann chuckled. "I know what you mean. Tell him I said hello when you see him. My dad's letting me help him in the clinic tomorrow. I get to assist him with real patients and everything."

Hank noticed she walked taller, and his smile widened for her. "Good for you. I'm sure you'll have more fun than we will in Smackover."

Daniel harrumphed. "What could be more fun than going to Smackover?"

"How about going to Smackover without having to work while we're there?"

"Oh, yeah, I guess you're right. But it's Smackover. I don't care if we have to work. I'm just happy to be going."

Beth Ann shifted her fishing pole and worm bucket to one hand and patted Daniel on his shoulder. "You can be excited about going to Smackover all you want, but I can hardly wait to finally do some real doctoring with my dad for a change. He's finally taking me seriously about being a doctor one day, even though I'm a girl."

As they reached the edge of the forest, Hank slowed and let his friends go on ahead. He glanced around for signs of others having made this same trek today.

"Come on, boys, daylight's wasting. I'll race you to the rock. The last one there has to give the winner his first fish."

Hank brought up the rear and watched Beth Ann run past Daniel. He didn't care if he lost, but the closer they got to their destination, the more his skin tingled. He slowed as images from this morning's dream filled his thoughts. The whoops and hollers of the other two snapped him out of his reverie.

It was just a dream, for goodness' sake.

He picked up his pace while he breathed in a deep breath through his nose and then blew it out through his mouth. He realized he needed to rub the nape of his neck but he couldn't because both hands were full. He stopped in the middle of the trail. A sense of foreboding and danger plagued him. He heard something in the trees just ahead. *Stop it! Daniel and Beth Ann are waiting on you. All you're doing is letting fear put things in your head.* He took a couple more steps then stopped. Hearing nothing out of the ordinary, he hiked on toward the fishing hole with deliberately steady steps until a bird swooped close to his face.

"Ahhh!" *Was that an owl or a buzzard? Doesn't matter!* Without looking to the right or left, he tore down the trail, making a beeline for the rock overlooking the river. His vision blurred momentarily. *Just follow the sound of Beth Ann's voice.* He skidded to a halt, nearly bumping into Daniel. He searched the trail behind him, and all merriment ended.

Chapter 3

Beth Ann dropped her gear and placed a hand on Hank's forearm. "What's wrong? You're shaking, and you look like you've seen a ghost."

Daniel gasped. Hank looked from one friend to the other as Beth Ann slapped her forehead. "Uh…okay. You both know I don't really believe in ghosts. Sorry, Daniel. It was a bad choice of words." She looked down the trail they had used. "But…"

Suddenly a loud crack disrupted the natural sounds in the woods. Then something thudded to the ground along the path just beyond their line of sight. "Never mind, I say we move from down here to up there."

Hank abandoned his pole and bucket of worms and joined Beth Ann as she dashed up the side of the rock overlooking their fishing hole. About halfway up, Hank heard Daniel's tackle hit the ground. With his peripheral vision Hank suppressed a nervous giggle as Daniel raced past and beat him and Beth Ann to the top. They all sat crossed-legged on the dusty, flat surface. Hank rested his head in his palms, his elbows jabbing his legs just above the knees. The sound of their heavy breathing struck his funny bone, as Daddy used to say. But he held it at bay as he assessed their situation.

"Well, I guess we won't be doing any fishing. All our gear is down there." He pointed toward the trail and then snorted as giggles refused to be denied anymore, and all three doubled over from uncontrolled hilarity. Before long, tears spilled down all their faces.

Beth Ann wiped her cheeks. "All right, now, I enjoy a good laugh like anyone else, but what was *that* all about? You should have seen your face, Hank." She guffawed till her face turned red as she held her sides. "Poor Daniel…"

Daniel snorted between chortles. "Hey…I may be slow…but I'm no fool…. He doesn't spook that easily. If he's scared…it's serious…." He wiped his brows with his shirtsleeves as he calmed down. "Did you feel one of those tingling things on the back of your neck? You know, like before?" He scratched the back of his own neck.

Hank's cheeks hurt. Heat flushed his face till it itched. He gazed down the trail toward home. "Yeah, actually I did, now that I think about it, but it was a bird…I think. It startled me, and…I ran." He sobered as the effect of dormant fears surfaced.

Daniel's face paled. His Adam's apple bobbed a couple of times. His eyebrows angled toward his hairline. The furrows in his forehead deepened; his demeanor became rigid. "Was it an owl? If it was, and you saw it in the daylight…you know what that means. You do, don't you?" He shuddered. "Or was it a buzzard? Those things are gosh-awful ugly, but they're bad luck, too. They eat dead things, and if you disturb one, you're in trouble. A buzzard puked on my cousin, Cliff, one time. Talk about nasty! Anyway, it's worse if it was just one buzzard. You really don't want to know what that means."

"Oh, brother, here we go again." Beth Ann chuckled.

Hank rolled his eyes as he stretched cramps from his sides. More giggles rumbled from deep within his abdomen. "Sorry, I'm not sure what kind of bird it was. I didn't even know it was there until it swooped down right in front of me. If I hadn't been carrying my fishing stuff, I might have been able to touch it. That's how close it was."

Daniel's voice cracked as it rose above the din of merriment. "That's not good at all. It's a sign. My grandma would call it an omen, the worst kind of sign."

Hank's mind flashed through the afternoon events as a more foreboding mind-set shrouded his mood.

Beth Ann stretched out her arms, palms opened toward the other two. "Okay, come on, guys, let's not get carried away with our imaginations. We've had a good laugh, but we need to calm down and think clearly." She sighed, and then rested her fists on her hips. "Why are you so jumpy all of a sudden, Hank? Like Daniel said, you don't scare easily. Is it your dream or something the sheriff said?"

He considered how much to tell his best friends as he worked the soreness out of his sides. He picked up a pebble and rolled it around in his palm. Then he tossed it over the edge of the rock, waiting to hear it plop into the river. "Al Higgins escaped from jail and may be coming here. The sheriff doesn't think I have anything to worry about, but I'm not so sure."

Daniel's forehead wrinkled with deep worry lines, again. "You think your kidnapper is coming after you?"

Beth Ann put her clasped hands on top of her head. "What makes you think you have something to worry about?"

"As soon as I heard he'd escaped with a couple of others, I knew *this* dream was like the others. I don't want these dreams, so why am I having them?"

Beth Ann pursed her lips and frowned. "Don't worry about the why right now. You have a gift. Just accept it and make use of the information they give you." She looked up and pointed to the sky overhead. "Someone up there is definitely looking out for you, just like the preacher talked about last Sunday. If you think about it, your dreams actually help us." She wrapped her arms around her knees. "When there's the possibility of danger, they give us the information we need to know what to do. That way, we're ready when the time comes. We need to get an idea of what we're up against. So let's hear it, and don't leave anything out." She reclined back on her hands, her arms straight.

Hank described every detail from his dream. "That's it. All of it." Then he shared what he knew about the escape and Uncle Will.

Daniel buried his clasped hands in the hole his bouncing, crisscrossed legs made. "I'd definitely say you're probably right. It's kind of a vision. In my opinion, we need to be prepared for three things that will happen."

The furrows between Hank's brows deepened. "What are you talking about? Three things…?"

Daniel moved his hands to his knees. "Yeah, my grandma is always talking about when bad things happen. She swears they come in threes. Even *I* have to admit she's right…most of the time. Then there's the omen of the owl or buzzard you saw this afternoon. That sort of verifies the coming events." He sat up tall. "Look, from what you just told us about your dream, I definitely see two things. If we go back over it, we'll probably see the third one. Here's what I can tell you for sure." He itemized his points on his fingers. "First, Al Higgins has escaped from jail with a couple of others and could be coming for you. Second, there's your missing brother from your dream. Higgins could be planning to kidnap him to get to you." His mouth made a small "o" as he sucked in a quick breath. "Oh, wow, I just thought of the third one." Hank recognized the twinkle in his eyes when he unraveled a mystery. "It's your Uncle Will. He was part of that whole mess, wasn't he? I'll bet his attack is somehow connected with the escape, for sure." He shrugged his shoulders. "And there you go, that makes three things." His fists framed his jaws. "Grandma's right…again." He slapped his knees as he blew air from his lungs and slumped, the sparkle gone from his eyes. "Doggone it."

After several seconds of silence, Beth Ann erupted into gut-wrenching laughter. "You actually believe that old wives' tale?

Come on, what would Sherlock Holmes say about your inclination to believe in silly superstitions? Where's the logic?"

Daniel's weak chuckle started a new wave of gaiety. "Did I mention that Grandma *swears* by it? I can't change the facts."

Relief calmed Hank's nervous stomach. "You two are the best. I really don't want to put either of you in danger, but I'm glad we talked. Whatever happens, if it's coming, I can't hide from it."

Beth Ann jabbed Daniel with her elbow. "Well, I'm up for a challenge to prove the error of thinking bad things happen in threes; and I, for one, am not going to let you go through this alone. We're a team. Let's keep it that way. How about it, are you with me on this, Mr. Holmes?"

"Sure. Just remember I warned you. Grandma is always right about these things."

"You said she was *almost* always right. This is going to be one of those times she's wrong." She offered her hands to them, initiating their special handshake to seal the pact.

Daniel grasped one of her forearms. "I'm definitely with you, but I have lots of history with Grandma. I'm not as sure as you are that she's wrong. We'll see."

Hank completed the circle. "I'm game, too. Thanks for sticking with me on this. I don't know what I'd do if I didn't have you two for friends."

Beth Ann broke away first. "Okay, enough mushy stuff. The team needs a plan. How do you want to deal with your dream?"

"Until something happens to *prove* it's real, there's nothing we can do. Once we know the escaped prisoners are in the area—*if* they're coming here—we can set a trap for them, maybe."

Daniel perked up. "What about Abraham? I bet he'll help."

Hank leaned back on his hands, his elbows locked. "We can ask him. I've been thinking a lot about his daddy's death lately. It's been nearly three months since we turned over the evidence we found to the sheriff. We need to find out if there's any progress on who killed him. I don't care if Mr. Blackman was a colored man. His death was a murder, and that's a crime that needs to be punished, no matter who did it. Color should never be an issue when laws are broken. Abraham deserves justice."

Beth Ann nodded. "I agree. I haven't heard anything from anyone around my dad's clinic, but I'll try to find out what I can tomorrow."

Daniel huffed. "There hasn't been *any* talk around town. It's like everyone has forgotten about it."

Hank sat up, wiping rock dust from his palms. "We can't let that happen. Maybe Mr. Pete will have some news. I'll ask him when he comes over for dinner tonight." Hank jerked his head up. "Oh, in all that's happened today, I forgot to tell you. The deputy asked Ma to marry him. They're getting married on the first of November before the potluck."

Daniel's eyebrows pointed toward his hairline. "You sound happy."

"I am."

"Then I am, too."

Beth Ann clasped her hands in front of her chest. "That's wonderful news. My dad really likes Deputy Collins. He's a good man, and he'll be a great father. I'm happy for you and your family."

Daniel scratched the top of his head. "My mom will *really* be glad to hear it. She's been talking about them getting married since he came to town. I think my dad was scared she'd…hey, wait a minute. Do you have any idea what this means?"

Hank frowned. "What?"

"That makes *four* things." Daniel's brows came together in a scowl. "I wonder what Grandma would say about that?"

"My ma marrying Mr. Pete is a good thing. I thought that old wives' tale had to do with bad news."

"Oh, yeah, you're right…huh—huh." His face reddened. "I just got a little carried away. Sorry."

"It's okay." The humor of the moment faded when Hank noticed the shadows lengthening toward the east. "Whoa, I just realized how late it is. I'll be in big trouble if I don't get home soon. Ma wasn't real happy about me coming out here after what the sheriff told us." They all climbed down from the rock and gathered their fishing gear. "I'll see you in the morning at my house, Daniel. Be there early. Mr. Pete wants to leave as soon after dawn as possible. I hope you have a good time with your dad at the clinic, Beth Ann." Hank resisted the urge to rub the back of his neck. "Let's get out of here before it gets dark."

* * * * * * *

An oppressing heaviness lifted from Hank's shoulders and chest as he ran out of the woods. He looked back before forcing himself to slow down as he walked across the field toward the backyard. The crisp nip in the autumn air burned his lungs and chilled his face. Thin wisps of white vapor escaped his mouth and nostrils as his breathing returned to a normal rhythm. He put his fishing gear in the green house where they kept the feed for the livestock, and then he put on his daddy's old blue checked flannel shirt hanging on a nail just inside the door. He wiped his nose on a sleeve and studied the sky.

Judging from the sun's position, there was about half an hour of good daylight left. He rushed to the barn to start his evening chores. When he finally shut the chickens in the hen house, the sun was just a sliver above the horizon. The evening star glowed against the backdrop of the yellows, oranges, pinks, purples, and various shades of blue of the sunset. He couldn't remember the last time he'd finished his chores so quickly.

The back door squeaked on its hinges when he opened it, and warm air rushed past him. He shrugged out of his daddy's shirt and hung it on a hook behind the door. He rubbed his hands together as he breathed in the aroma of baking ham, and his stomach growled. "Hey, Jimmy Jack, I mean, Jimmy. Where's Ma? When's supper going to be ready?"

His younger brother sat at the kitchen table working on his arithmetic homework. "I think she's taking a nap. I don't know about supper."

Hank's heart hammered against his ribs as he tiptoed down the hall. *Something's wrong. She hasn't taken a nap before putting supper on the table since...*

Chapter 4

Hank heard a soft sob come from his ma's bedroom, where the door stood ajar. The emotional shell around his heart shattered into a thousand pieces. He hesitated a moment before entering and winced as the creaking of the floor reverberated off the walls. Ma sat in the rocking chair Daddy had made her, facing the dusky darkness outside the window.

He cleared his throat. "I'm sorry, Ma. I didn't mean to make you cry. I should have told you when I got back from the river. It's just that I wanted to do my chores before dark."

She blew her nose and wiped her eyes. "Oh, no, son, come on in. I'm not crying because of you or anything you did. It…I just needed a moment to myself. I should have paid closer attention to the time."

"I was worried when I didn't see you getting supper ready like usual."

"I know, and I'm sorry. I didn't mean to make you fret." Her voice trembled as she spoke, and she sniffed before blowing her nose.

"Is there news about Uncle Will? Is he…"

"No." She stood and turned toward him, her eyes red and her lips quivering.

"What's wrong, then?" As he sat on the bed, he detected her new engagement ring on the nightstand. "Are you worried about the wedding? Did something happen between you and..."

She reached for her ring and studied it. "No...sweetie, it's..." She slid it on her finger and smiled.

"Are you having second thoughts about marrying Mr. Pete? It's okay if you are. You don't have to marry him just because of me and Jimmy."

She sat beside Hank, putting an arm around his shoulders and squeezing. "I was just thinking about your dad, missing him." She wiped her eyes and cheeks with one of her embroidered handkerchiefs. "I really don't know where these emotions are coming from. I thought I was done with the crying, until..."

"Until you told Mr. Pete you'd marry him?"

She pulled a second handkerchief from her apron pocket and blew her nose. "Yeah, but..."

"If you don't love him, don't go through with it."

"You're growing up so fast, son. You make me so proud, and you guard your father's memory so honorably. Your concern warms my heart, but it's not at all what you're thinking. I'm not marrying Pete just so you boys will have a father. I *do* love him. It's just that I realized today how much I still love your father, too. I didn't think I could love another man like I did...do him..."

Hank nodded. "I understand, sort of. Have you talked with Mr. Pete about this?"

She shook her head, and he watched her hands smooth her tear-stained handkerchief across her lap. "No, it just came to me this afternoon." She sighed.

"You can talk to him, Ma. He needs to know what you're feeling. I didn't mean to pry. I was just concerned because you're never late getting supper on the table except when you're sad, and what with you crying and all…I hope you're okay."

She grinned as she ruffled his hair, the tension in the room breaking. "I love your compassion, you know that? You are so very much like your daddy." She folded her hands in her lap. "Forgive me for burdening you. You're just a boy, and I don't know what came over me telling you about all of this. I'll talk to Pete tonight." She breathed in deeply and exhaled slowly. "You needn't worry about me. I'm fine. Now, how about some supper. Are you hungry? It's mostly done already. I just need to glaze the ham, make some cornbread, and mash the potatoes." They stood at the same time. She looked at her ring again and smiled.

Hank hugged her. "I love you, Ma."

"I love you, too, my young prince." She kissed the top of his head.

Hank smiled and breathed in her perfume. "You haven't called me that in a long time." Then his mood sobered, and he looked up at her. "You know, I still think about him a lot. Honestly? My heart hurts because I love him so much, and I know he's gone. If it weren't for Mr. Pete, I don't know if I would be able to get past missing him. He helps me put it all in perspective."

"He's a good man. I think your father would approve of my marrying him. Pete loves you boys…"

"And you, Ma."

She chuckled. "Yes…and me. It's almost like your daddy's home again, isn't it? Almost, but…"

"Yeah, I know."

She stepped to the mirror, looking at her reflection. "Well, I'd better…"

Without warning, someone pounded on the front door.

"Who in the world…?" Ma blew her nose once more before pinching her cheeks and patting her hair. She smoothed her skirt as she left the room, but Hank's feet refused to move.

Jimmy shouted from the back of the house. "I'll get it." When Hank heard the chair scrape across the kitchen floor, an instant replay of the sheriff's visit flashed through his thoughts. He scrambled into the hallway and reached for Ma's hand.

"Wait. What if it's…?" He swallowed hard as his pulse thundered in his ears, unable to finish his question. A tingling heat flooded his body. Her forehead wrinkled, and her eyes opened wider.

"I'll get it." Jimmy plowed into Hank, pushing him into Ma.

"Hey…." He pushed his little brother away from him.

Ma put a hand on each of their shoulders. "Oh, no, you won't, not this time. You boys stay back, you hear." She waited until they both nodded, and then left them where they stood.

"Sorry about running into you. Is something wrong? She looks worried."

Hank took a moment to calm his panicked voice and put an arm around Jimmy's shoulders. "Just watch where you're going. You aren't the only one in the house, you know." He rubbed the top of his brother's head with his knuckles. "Come on. Let's see who's here, but stay back like she said."

"Okay."

They rushed to the parlor, stopping abruptly when Ma glowered at them just as they cleared the hall. She opened the door, but no one stood on the other side. As she stepped outside, the brothers dashed after her. Hank almost tumbled down the porch steps as he scanned the yard. It took several seconds for his eyes to adjust as dusk dissolved into darkness. He heard his brother run across the length of the porch behind him.

Ma walked the perimeter of the porch. "That's strange. Why would someone pound on our door like that then leave? Oh, well, whoever knocked is gone now. Pete will be here soon. I'll have him look around. Right now, I need to get supper on the table. You boys come on in. It's getting dark and cold. I don't want you out here by yourselves. I have enough to worry about without adding you two to everything else from today."

Hank turned toward the house. "You heard her, Jimmy. Let's go inside." As he climbed the steps to the porch, something caught his attention. *Is that a note?* Someone had tacked a piece of paper with dark writing on it to one of the posts at the top of the porch steps. Everything moved in slow motion. *When was that put there?* He was careful not to alarm his brother.

Jimmy stood at the top of the steps, hugging the column several inches above the mysterious note.

"She *is* worried. What's going on?"

He forced himself to breathe and sound normal. "If she had wanted us to know, she would have told us." The edges of the paper curled in the breeze. He looked at the sweet gum tree, recalling the details from his dream. Swallowing past the dryness of his opened mouth, he tried to squash the fear threatening to overcome his ability to think. "You need to get inside, little brother."

"What about you? Aren't you coming inside, too?"

"Yeah, I just want to check on something real quick."

"But…"

"Go on, now. I'll only be a minute."

He heard the screen door slam shut, but not the front door. He watched Jimmy skip down the hall toward the kitchen, and then he rolled his eyes and shook his head. *That boy must have been born in the barn.* He slipped across the porch and twisted the knob to close the big door, careful to be quiet. He muffled the noise of the screen shutting, but cringed as the hinges squeaked from the cold. Then he turned his attention back to the paper and hoped no one else had seen it. He snatched it into his fist and stuffed it into his right front pants pocket. *I'll read this later.*

He sprinted to the end of the porch, looking across the open field at the side of the house, and jumped. When his feet hit the ground, a sharp pain jolted up both legs. A chill washed over him, so he cupped his fists and blew into them. He looked past his bedroom window, toward the garden area, and forced himself to stay calm. *Whoever left that note has to still be here, but where?* He turned in a circle as he studied the landscape between the woods and the Baker house. As he looked toward the back of the property and the road to Granny Rose's place, he saw someone set something large against the side of the barn. Hank's heart slammed against his chest until he realized the shadowy figure looked extremely large and tall. *Mr. Morgan?* Then he noticed the person had a limp. *Yep, it's Mr. Morgan. I wonder where he's headed this time.* He took comfort in his big Indian friend's presence, even though he shivered as much from adrenaline as from the cold.

The man stood almost eight feet tall, but he was as gentle-spirited as they came. Jeffrey Morgan was something of a mystery and a curious fellow who stayed close to Granny Rose for some reason. He didn't talk about himself much, but he had saved Hank and his friends on more than one occasion since his arrival this past summer. He didn't need to know any more about the man to call him a loyal friend.

"Mr. Morgan." His teeth chattered as he wrapped his arms around himself, unsure he could be heard, much less understood.

The man waved. He covered the fifty yards between the barn and the house in a matter of seconds with his six-foot walking stride. "Hello, my young friend. What are you doing out here in the cold without a coat?"

"Someone pounded on our door like it was important, but when Ma opened it, no one was there. I was looking around for whoever it could have been. You didn't happen to see anything or pass anyone on your way over here, did you?"

"No, and I'm alone."

The familiar tingle started at the nape of Hank's neck and spread to his scalp. "What brings you out this way? Are you going somewhere?" He nodded toward the barn.

The big man looked behind him, and then down at Hank. "Yeah, I am, but I couldn't leave without coming by here first."

"How long are you going to be gone this time?"

"I'm not sure."

"You'll be back, won't you?"

"I'm not sure."

"But…"

"I have some unfinished business to take care of. I don't know how it will turn out, but I need to settle up with you and your family before I go, just in case I don't return."

"Settle up? I don't understand."

"You've been very kind to me, but I'm afraid I haven't been totally honest with you. I came here to keep a promise to a friend. I owe him that, at least. I need to finish what I came here to do. Then I'll know where I belong. Come on, let's go in so I can get this over with."

Every nerve pricked Hank's shoulders, neck, and scalp. His skin burned where the man's huge hand draped over his shoulder, and his heartbeat pounded in his ears.

As they walked toward the front yard, the sheriff's words echoed in his brain. *Oh, no. Surely Mr. Morgan isn't in cahoots with Mr. Higgins.* A dull ache spread through his abdomen with each step he took. Lights from a motor car briefly spotlighted them as it came up the driveway. They stood at the foot of the porch steps. *Mr. Pete.*

"Looks like I'll be back after all. I've waited this long. Another day or two won't matter. We'll talk after I take care of some personal business out of town."

The cold night air permeated every pore the giant's hand had covered on Hank's shoulder. When he turned around, the Indian had already left, taking whatever he had leaned against the barn with him.

Chapter 5

Everything spun in slow motion as Hank processed the conversation with Mr. Morgan and the man's rush to leave as soon as the deputy arrived. Every nerve in Hank's body shook. The dizziness subsided. Then his Achilles heel brushed against a porch step. He sat hard on the second step up to avoid collapsing in a heap. He shook his head. *No, you're letting your imagination run away with you. He's a friend. Think about it.*

"Was that Mr. Morgan I saw just now?" Mr. Pete's voice came from a long tunnel until he stood right in front of Hank. "More importantly, what are you doing out here in the cold...alone?"

Hank stood, shoving his hands into his pants pockets. His right fist crumpled the paper he had stuffed there several minutes ago. "Waiting on you." He nodded toward the house. "You said you wanted to know if something strange happened. Well, it did. Someone pounded on the front door just as it was getting dark. When Ma opened it, whoever had been there was gone."

"That was Jeffrey Morgan I saw with you just now, wasn't it?"

"Yes sir."

"Was he the one who had knocked?"

"He said it wasn't."

"Hmmm." Mr. Pete's brows furrowed, as he stood with his feet shoulder width apart, his arms akimbo. He scanned the perimeter of the yard. "Did you notice anything out of the ordinary around the yard?"

Hank felt the edge of the note in his pocket. "I was just starting to check things out when I saw Mr. Morgan. When I asked, he said he hadn't seen anyone or anything. We were about to go in when you drove up, and then he left in a big hurry."

"Did he say why he was here?"

The nerves just under the skin of Hank's face and scalp pricked like tiny pins and needles. He squeezed his fists, his fingernails stabbing his palms. *Don't scratch.* His chin quivered in the cold night air, making him stutter. "Not really. He's leaving again, but he said he'd be back in a few days."

The deputy blew into his fists. "Okay, you need to get inside and warm up. Tell your ma I'll be in after I take a look around."

"Yes sir."

* * * * * * *

The smell of purple-hull peas boiled with salt pork, hot water cornbread, buttery mashed potatoes, and baked ham glazed with honey and brown sugar filled the house. While Jimmy finished setting the table, Hank helped Ma put food on the table. After pouring sweet milk into four glasses, he returned the half-empty pitcher to the icebox. The noise of stomping feet on the back porch thundered through the kitchen just before the back door opened. A chill rushed into the house as the deputy shut it again. He shrugged out of his coat and hung it on the hook behind the door, rubbing his hands together and blowing on them.

"Whew, the Almanac was dead on right, again. A cold front is definitely moving in. The temperature is dropping fast out there. There could be a light frost on the ground in the morning, the first one of the season. But I wouldn't count Indian summer out just yet. It's still too early for the cold to settle in till spring according to the Almanac...and Granny." He gave Ma a quick kiss. "Honey, everything looks to be okay as far as I can tell in the dark. I'll check again in the morning before we head to Smackover, just to be sure I didn't overlook anything." He pumped water at the sink. "Supper sure smells good."

"You're just in time. It's ready to eat."

Even though his voice had sounded normal, Hank noticed the worry lines between the man's brows as he washed up. *Something's bothering him. He looks just like Daddy did when he was troubled but didn't want to upset Ma. I need to read the note before...*

"Hank? Are you going to join us?"

"Sorry, Ma." Hank's cheeks burned. He was the only one still standing. He sat across from Mr. Pete.

They all held hands during grace, closing the circle as Daddy used to say. Hank peeked at the deputy as he voiced the prayer. *He could be you, Daddy, but I know he isn't. It's comforting, though, you know?* He closed his eyes just before the "Amen."

As the plate of ham was passed around the table, he made brief eye contact with the man who would soon be his stepfather. Hank's stomach rumbled and growled as he served himself, remembering he had only eaten part of Beth Ann's fried pie since breakfast. Until now, he hadn't really thought about being hungry.

Ma chuckled. "Well, someone's hungry."

Hank was grateful when Jimmy's loud sigh drew attention away from himself.

"What's wrong, little man?"

Jimmy sniffed without looking up, taking a bite of peas and cornbread. "I'm not little anymore, Ma."

She smiled. "I'll try to remember that, hon. And you remember your manners. It's not polite to talk with your mouth full."

He swallowed. "Yes ma'am." He put his left elbow on the table, cradling his head in his hand. With his other hand, he twirled his fork in his potatoes before putting some in his mouth. He swallowed before speaking. "I'm just wondering when I'll be able to do things with Mr. Pete and Hank, like everyone else."

Ma sighed. "Manners, son. Elbow off the table. Sit up tall so your food will digest properly." He complied. "Thank you. Now, what's this? You don't like being with me anymore?"

"It's not that. I just wish I didn't have to stay home all the time while Hank gets to do things like go to Smackover. He's *always* doing something with *everyone* except me. I'll never be old enough or big enough."

Mr. Pete swallowed a mouthful of food, and then took a drink of his milk. "You know, Jimmy, it's not easy being the older brother. Believe me, Hank has his own issues. Your time will come." After taking a couple of bites of vegetables, he sat back in his chair and rested his forearms on either side of his plate. "Um, sweetheart, I might have a solution for Jimmy and his humdrum life...for tomorrow, at least. Why don't you and the boys gather up some things after supper and come with me to Granny's tonight. Then you and Jimmy won't be here alone, and he can have his own adventures there while we're away. I'm sure Abraham won't mind me bunking with him in the barn tonight." The deputy got up and retrieved the pitcher of buttermilk from the icebox.

Ma's brows furrowed. "I don't know. I really don't like inviting myself or imposing on her."

Mr. Pete crumbled a large piece of cornbread into his empty glass, and then he added some buttermilk, stirring it together. "You aren't inviting yourself, and you're not imposing. After bringing Jimmy home from school, I checked in on her and told her about Stan's visit. When I shared my concerns with her, she agreed with me." He licked his spoon. "We really need to make this trip to Smackover. We've put it off almost too long as it is. It was actually her idea to invite you all over to spend the night."

The deputy took hold of Ma's hand and kissed it. "You know Granny. She's a proud Indian who won't admit when she needs help. And she knows I worry about her since her heart attack. I've noticed she's moving a bit slower the last couple of days. I don't think it's all because of the change in the weather, either. I think the situation here gave her the perfect reason to have someone with her while we're in Smackover without having to admit anything to me." He chuckled as he scooped a spoonful of buttermilk soaked cornbread from his glass. "She made me promise not to pressure you." His smile faded after he swallowed. "But I have to say, though, it would make me feel a lot better knowing you were there instead of here, especially after your visitor tonight." Deputy Collins caressed her shoulder. "What do you say?"

Hank noticed the deputy's brows furrow slightly as he spoke. *I knew it. He's worried about who was at the door. I need to read the note.*

Jimmy did his happy dance in his chair. When he spoke, the melancholy from earlier was gone. "Yeah, Ma. You heard him. It's a great idea, and Granny *wants* us to come. Please say yes. Please?" He clasped prayerful hands and gave her a snaggle-toothed grin. "It'll be like we're taking a trip, too."

Mr. Pete chuckled as he ruffled his hair. "You'd like that?"

"Yeah, I would. Hank always gets to do fun stuff. I never get to."

"Hey, that's not true."

"Please, Ma?"

"What do you say, honey? Granny said I couldn't pressure you." The deputy scooped another spoonful of cornbread and buttermilk, nodding in Jimmy's direction. "She didn't say *he* couldn't. Besides, we can't let Hank have all the fun, now can we?" He drank the last bit of crumbs and milk from his glass.

Ma quietly stood with her hand poised to take her plate away, but her eyes were closed as she breathed slowly in and out. After a brief moment, she took her plate to the sink. No one spoke. The sound of forks and knives scraping plates as everyone at the table continued eating set Hank's nerves on edge. After Ma washed her dishes and dried her hands on her apron, she faced the family. She leaned against the counter and clasped her hands in front of her.

Hank knew the look in her eyes all too well. "Fine. We'll go *this* time. Now, finish your supper and save room for dessert."

All conversation stopped for the moment. Ma swapped empty plates with bowls of warm peach cobbler all around the table. Hank's mouth watered in anticipation. This summer's crop was the sweetest since Daddy left for the war. With everyone having been served dessert, she sat without speaking, somewhat hesitant.

"What's wrong, sweetheart?"

She looked at Mr. Pete. Worry lines stretched across her forehead. "I don't want to make a habit of running to Granny's whenever there's...whenever you're out of town."

"Why not?" Then the deputy winked at her, and they both smiled.

Hank felt the tension in the room dissolve. Jimmy wiggled in his seat as he finished his cobbler.

The deputy patted Ma's hands before covering them with both of his. "Look, I understand your hesitation, and I respect your concerns." Hank recognized the serious tone in the deputy's voice. "It's just that the special circumstances this time warrant caution. I love you, and I want you safe."

Jimmy slammed his empty milk glass on the table and burped. "Excuse me." His brows came together. "Mr. Pete, what's really going on? Why are you and Ma worried?" A hush filled the room. All activity stopped for several seconds.

"What makes you think something's wrong?"

"It's kind of obvious. She's behaving like when Daddy didn't come home from the war. Then when you and Ma talk, you're careful about what you say and how you say it. From the way Hank's acting, I'm pretty sure he knows, so why can't I? I'm almost ten, you know."

Mr. Pete shifted in his seat and set his napkin beside his empty dessert bowl. He clasped his hands together on the table in front of him. "You're very observant. You'd make a good police officer.

Your ma and I haven't discussed when to tell you, but since you're asking, we'll talk now. I don't want you to worry, though, because everything is going to be okay. You also need to understand there will be times we won't tell *either* of you boys things because they don't concern you. It's not keeping secrets from you. It's just taking care of business where it belongs. Okay?"

Jimmy scraped his dessert bowl with his spoon one last time before giving it to Ma. "Yes sir." Then he copied the deputy's posture as he listened. Mr. Pete and Ma took turns sharing general information about the situation with the trial and Uncle Will. Hank lost track of the conversation, distracted by the note in his pocket. Before he could excuse himself from the table, Ma stood.

"Well, boys, why don't you get some things packed for *one* night at Granny's while Pete and I clean the kitchen. Don't take too long. It's getting late, and I don't want to keep her up waiting for us." The noise of chair legs scraping against the floor announced the end of supper. Hank's heart hammered against his chest. *Now, maybe I can read the note.* He planned to beat Jimmy to the bedroom, but he changed his mind when he heard his little brother's distressed voice.

"Ma, I'm sad about Uncle Will, but I'm really scared for Hank."

Hank gripped the back of his chair, his knuckles white as he pushed it under the table. His pulse roared in his ears. His brother's shoulders shook as Ma wrapped him in a hug and rubbed his back. "It's okay, baby. We'll just keep praying for Uncle Will like we have been and ask God to heal his wounds, too. Don't worry about Hank, either. God will watch over him *and* us. Why do you think he brought Pete into our lives?"

Hank flexed his fists as blood flowed again to his fingers. "Come on, little brother. Let's get packed. But first, I have a question for you."

Jimmy wiped his eyes with his shirtsleeve and sniffed a couple of times. "What's your question?"

Hank put his arm around his brother's shoulders as they left the kitchen. "Do you know how we can get in touch with the Golden Eagle? I think we need him to keep a watch out for those escaped prisoners." Jimmy smiled as they headed toward their bedroom. Hank looked back once. He noticed Ma's eyes were shiny as she mouthed "thank you." He nodded.

"Really?"

"Yeah."

Jimmy talked nonstop down the hallway about his hero, the Golden Eagle. He was *all* Jimmy talked about lately. He bragged about his ability to run fast and reach the tops of trees like he could fly. It was by chance Hank found out his brother was actually his own hero when Hank found his costume, one of Ma's petticoats, under his bed one night. They packed as he listened to Jimmy talk on and on about his special friend with extraordinary abilities. Something resembling warm spring water washed over Hank's soul.

He sounds like me talking about you, Daddy. I just wish he could remember you. I'm glad he loves Mr. Pete, though. I didn't like it at first, but he needs someone like you to admire, especially when he outgrows the Golden Eagle. I understand it now. While I have you, he has Mr. Pete.

The knock on their bedroom door startled Hank. He bit his tongue to keep from yelling as Ma stuck her head around the door.

"Come on, boys. Pete's waiting for us outside. What's taking you so long?" She left the door open when she left.

"I wish we could stay more than just one night."

"You're lucky she said we could go tonight. Go on, now. I'll be right behind you."

When Jimmy left the room, Hank stole a quick moment to read the note. He pulled the crumpled piece of paper from his pocket. His hands shook as he smoothed out the wrinkles. His knees buckled as the blood drained from his face.

Chapter 6

Hank sat on the edge of his bed and stared at the note. In bold, blocked letters, someone had printed the message:

LIKE FATHER, LIKE SON.

The deputy called from the front parlor. "Hank, let's go. Your ma is getting annoyed. What are you doing?"

Hank jumped, ripping the note in two, and quickly shoved the pieces back in his pants pocket. He stuffed his arms into the sleeves of his duster and left. "Coming, Mr. Pete." Just outside his bedroom door, the two collided. "Humph..."

"Whoa, slow down there. I know your ma's anxious to leave, but we have plenty of time before Granny sends out a search party for us."

"Sorry, I didn't realize you were there."

"No problem. Let's just go before your ma changes her mind, how about it?"

* * * * * * *

The rooms in Granny's house were much larger than at the Baker house. She had two full-sized beds in the middle bedroom alone, with lots of standing room besides. *So this is the room Daniel swears is haunted.* Hank grinned and shook his head. *Where does he come up with that stuff? You make me laugh, Daniel.* Hank's shoulders sagged as he blew out of long sigh. *I just hope I can sleep after the day I've had today.* He carried a lit oil lamp with one hand and his packed carpetbag with the other. His brother joined him at the door while he let his eyes adjust to the dimly lit room.

Jimmy's bag fell to the floor with a thud. "Look at the size of those beds. They're as high off the floor as they are wide, I'll bet. Which one do you want?"

"Which one do you think? Same as at home." He set the lamp on the dresser near the door on his left, and then tossed his bag across the room. It landed in the middle of the bed nearest the windows.

"Nice toss."

"Thanks."

Jimmy Jack ran and leaped up on the bed in the corner, which stood at the foot of Hank's, and then he bounced a couple of times on it. "Soft, just like I like it. What about yours?"

"It'll be fine. Let's turn in." Hank blew out the lamp then used the moonlight to guide him to his chosen bed. "I need to get some sleep, so no more talking. Tomorrow's going to be a long day."

The sheets smelled like sunshine and starch. They were cool to the touch, but once the down-filled mattress wrapped around him Hank knew he would be well insulated from the cold. With the nine-foot ceiling, no fireplace, and the likelihood of an early morning frost, it would be toasty warm under the covers.

It didn't take Jimmy long to start snoring, but it didn't bother Hank. It was as normal as the other nighttime noises around the house. What amazed him was how his brother could be wide awake one moment and sound asleep the next. Tonight, he hoped his *own* eyes would stay shut.

A maelstrom of thoughts flooded his brain. *How am I supposed to sleep when my mind won't shut off?* Besides the note, the dream and Daniel's remark about bad things happening in threes kept him awake. He turned over and gazed at the night sky. The moon was just above the treetops in the distance. The view usually soothed him so he went to sleep quickly, but not tonight. *If Daniel's right, the dream, the prison break, and Uncle Will's attack make three. But wait...these three are linked, aren't they? Does that mean they're all one instead of three? If so, that means there are two more...oh, brother, now he's got me doing it.*

Then his spinning thoughts landed on the note. As he considered the message, the skeleton he had found before his kidnapping flashed across his memory. *Abraham's murdered daddy? Where did that come from?* He sat up in bed. *Oh, that's just great! I forgot to ask Mr. Pete about Mr. Blackman's case.* He lay back down and sighed before turning on his side and pulling the covers up to his ears.

Hank recalled every detail of the discovery. He had secretly accepted the personal challenge and responsibility of identifying the person who had been shot and strapped to a tree near the river. With the help of Daniel and Beth Ann, he learned the body was their Negro friend's missing father—George Washington Blackman. Hank was determined to see Abraham and his family got the justice the law required for such a heinous crime, in spite of their skin color. They deserved to know what had happened just as much as Hank and his family had deserved to know what had happened to Daddy when he went missing. Hank made Deputy Collin promise to keep the investigation from being buried or forgotten. All of a sudden, Hank sat up in bed, again. Sweat beaded along his hairline, but not from the mattress.

What if I was wrong? "Like father, like son." What if the note isn't about Daddy and me? What if it's about Abraham and his daddy? That definitely makes more sense, especially if the murderer is a white man. Abraham's a loose end. The murderer would rather kill Abraham than go to prison. So why did I get the note? Hank lay back on his down-filled pillow. Hundreds of tiny pins pricked his heart. He heard Beth Ann's voice from earlier in the day. *You have a gift.*

The pit of his stomach roiled. *She's right. Like it or not, I have a gift. I must have passed some sort of test with the first dream in June, and now I'm stuck with them. Thanks a lot, God. I was trying to prove to Ma I can be the man of the house while Daddy was away, but you've cursed me.* His mouth watered as he felt pressure push under his chin. He needed to keep his food down, so he swallowed past his body's unique warning trigger for being sick.

Just then, Granny's grandfather clock struck the first of twelve deep-toned chimes, startling Hank out of his reverie. He counted each bong, not the least bit sleepy. *Great, just great! Three hours! I've been lying here awake for three stinking hours! I need to get some rest.* He turned away from the window and burrowed deeper into the mattress, covering his head and hoping for a dreamless sleep.

* * * * * * *

Hank couldn't stop yawning through breakfast. He didn't taste any of the grits, honey biscuits, bacon, and eggs Granny and Ma had served him. His vision swirled as he tried to focus on eating. It felt like he had just gone to sleep when Mr. Pete shook him awake. It was still dark when he got up, but dawn was breaking the eastern sky before he was dressed. Now he could barely stay awake long enough to eat.

"Hey, sleepy-head. Wake up." Mr. Pete chuckled as Hank's propping hand jerked out from under his cheek. He wiped his wet palm on his trousers then dried his chin on his shirtsleeve.

He must have gotten a good night's sleep. No one should be so cheerful this early in the morning.

"Sorry. I guess I need to splash some more cold water on my face."

The deputy sat across from him as he ate his own breakfast. "Better eat all of that. It'll be a while before we have lunch in Smackover. You might want to get a hat from home, too, before we head out. It's a bit nippy outside this crisp, frosty, autumn morning." He grinned and took his empty plate to Granny. Then he ruffled Hank's hair before he reached for his own duster and hat hanging behind the back door. "Come on, now. I'll help with your chores while Abraham does them around here. We don't want to get a late start for Smackover or we'll be late getting back. Finish your breakfast. Meet me out back in ten minutes. Since we'll be bringing the wagon back, we'll walk. Let's take the shortcut. That should wake you up." The deputy kissed the women then went out to the backyard.

Hank sopped the last bit of sunny-side-up eggs and grits with his biscuit, and then stuffed it in his mouth. He chewed fast as he put his empty plate in the wash water and grabbed several slices of bacon and a biscuit from the table, wrapping them in his napkin. "I love these biscuits and bacon. Good breakfast. See you all tonight." He shrugged into his duster then kissed Granny and Ma on their cheeks. "Love you. Bye." He almost forgot to shut the door quietly as he rushed to catch up with Mr. Pete.

* * * * * * *

Hank definitely needed his hat. His ears stung, so he covered them the best he could with the collar of his duster. He was glad Mr. Pete had thought to bring the lantern. The woods were still dark, even though daylight was spreading across the sky in earnest. They didn't talk much except to decide on which chores each of them would do when they got to the Baker property. As far as Hank was concerned, it was too early to hold an intelligent conversation.

With only the crunch and thud of their boots along the path between Granny's place and the Baker farm, Hank's mind charged into a deliberation of the connection between the contents of the note and Abraham. As if it were definitely true, he wondered how this new revelation measured up to Daniel's three events theory.

Is there any truth to that old wives' tale? It was uncanny how the dream, the prison break, and Uncle Will's attack seemed to be related *and* added up to three. *Do the events have to be related? What about the note?* Then Hank remembered Al Higgins, Harry Sawyer, and the stranger who left the note last night. *What's the connection with those three? Is there a connection? What about Uncle Will? He was in on the kidnapping scheme with Mr. Higgins and Mr. Sawyer. Then there's Mr. Morgan's mysterious behavior and his strange promise.* No matter how much Hank wanted to believe in their friendship, a nagging doubt tainted the absolute certainty of his relationship with the one he thought was a gentle giant.

Just as they cleared the woods, a chill shook Hank. He kept looking back over his shoulders while walking toward the barn. He absently rubbed the nape of his neck until he realized what he was doing. Then he stopped in his tracks and looked at his hand. He turned and stared at the woods between the Baker property and Granny's for several seconds. *Someone's watching us.*

"Hey, what are you looking at? Time's wasting. Let's get these chores done and hitch the mules to the wagon."

Trust your heart and not your eyes. Act wisely because there will be times you'll need to trust your eyes and not your heart.

The voice was in his head, but the words *sounded* like they had come from behind him, toward the barn. Then it was all gone—the voice, the words, and the tingle where his neck and hairline met.

"Hank."

Huh? "Yeah. Coming."

* * * * * * *

About half an hour later, with Mr. Pete sitting beside him, Hank drove the wagon from the barn to the driveway beside the house. Toby and Daisy May shook their heads, rattling their bridles, and stamped their front hooves.

"You told Daniel to be here early, didn't you?"

"Yes sir."

Just then, Hank's best friend came running around the bend and up to the Baker house.

"Here he comes."

Deputy Collins chuckled when the boy stopped running. He jumped down from his seat beside Hank and waited for Daniel. "Morning. Glad you finally made it. This trip wouldn't have been the same without you."

"Morning. Whew, glad I didn't miss you. I thought I'd never get over here."

Hank grinned, happy to see his best friend. He watched Mr. Pete lace his fingers together into a stirrup for Daniel to use to climb over the side and into the back of the wagon.

"Up you go. Are you all right? You look winded."

"Yes sir. I've been rushing around since I got up. I was afraid I'd have to run all the way to Granny's. It's been one of those kinds of mornings. I just need a minute to catch my breath." He lay on his back with his arm over his forehead, his chest heaving. "If it could go wrong at home, it did. I had to chase some chickens back into the chicken yard after fixing the hole they'd made. Then something spooked the cow, and she wouldn't let me milk her. Ma had to finally come out and take over the milking so I could leave. I just hope it's not a sign of what we can expect the rest of the day to be like."

Mr. Pete chuckled as he took his seat again. "Well, let's not borrow trouble where there isn't any. Instead, let's decide right now to turn this day around for you and enjoy our time together. Hank, how about you two take this wagon. Abraham and I will take Granny's. You have your list?"

"Yes sir. Daniel and I will follow you and Abraham, if that's okay."

"Sounds good. I thought you were going to get your hat. Your ears are really red."

"Oh, yeah. I'll be right back." Hank set the brake and wrapped the reins around the lever before jumping down and running into the house. When he shut the front door behind him, the hair on the back of his neck bristled. "Hello? Is someone here?" He listened without moving for several seconds. Then he stepped lightly through the hallway to his bedroom, as if he were trying not to wake Ma or Jimmy.

When he entered his room, he saw the window was closed and everything was in its place. Yet... *Something's not right.* Then he noticed the new hat he'd been wearing lately wasn't on the hook where he kept it. His knees trembled. *Someone's been in the house since we left last night.* Nothing else looked out of place. *No, you're letting your imagination get to you again. You probably left it at school when you came home early yesterday. Don't borrow trouble where there is none. Figure it out later. They're waiting on you.*

He went to the closet and found his old hat on the top shelf. He slapped it against his leg and checked it for spiders before putting it on, forcing himself to walk out of the house and act normal. *No need to sound an alarm until I'm sure there's a reason for it.* He secured the front door and heard the screen slam as he ran back to the wagon. *Remember what Daddy used to say? Trust your instincts. What are they telling you about what just happened? Something's not right. But without evidence...*

Mr. Pete's voice shattered his concentration. "Everything all right?"

Chapter 7

Hank tripped on a tree root. "Yes sir." *Careful. Don't raise suspicion without cause.* He climbed up into the driver's seat and laced the reins around his fingers.

"Good. Let's go. Abraham's waiting for us, and daylight's burning. Mr. Byrd has cleaned up Smackover quite a bit since becoming mayor, but being on the road we have to take at night is still pretty dangerous."

Hank released the brake and slapped the mules' rumps with the reins. He set all else aside in his mind for now and focused on the trip.

"Do you know if there's still a Death Valley, Mr. Pete?"

"I don't know if there is or not, but it really doesn't matter. As far as your ma is concerned, there is, and it stretches all the way to Farmville. She's the one who'll worry until we get back."

"Yeah, you're right about that."

Daniel stuck his head between the two on the bench, resting his forearms on the back rest. "Hey, Deputy, won't we pass Peanut Hill? That's where Mother King lived, isn't it? What was her business called?"

Mr. Pete cocked one eyebrow up and looked at Daniel without speaking for several seconds. "I have to say that's one place I'm glad burned to the ground. We still don't know what really happened to it. But believe me, the last place you wanted to stop was the U Auto Stop. Why the interest?"

"Curiosity. We will pass it, won't we?"

"You know what they say, don't you? Curiosity *killed* the cat."

Hank grinned as his best friend pointed toward the sky. "Ah, but satisfaction brought him back." Then he quickly raised and lowered his eyebrows a couple of times. They all laughed. Hank enjoyed his friend's sense of humor as much as he admired his deductive skills.

Mr. Pete shifted in his seat, facing the front. "Yes, we will be going by her place, what's left of it, but we won't be stopping."

Daniel chuckled until the deputy looked at him again with one eyebrow raised higher than the other. They turned onto Granny's driveway at the same time Abraham drove her wagon out of the barn. They parked side by side under the sweet gum tree across from her front yard. Hank set the brake and jumped down after Daniel and Mr. Pete. The deputy went inside for a few minutes while the boys talked about what they wanted to see before they left Smackover, if time permitted.

It was Abraham's first trip to the most famous and infamous oil town ever, as Hank remembered reading one reporter's take on the area's boom. He had saved the article to use in a report for school when he got the chance. His own reporter curiosity had already scooped up as much information about the tiny town as he could find and had it all filed away for future reference.

Smackover went from just about a hundred in population to more than 25,000 in just a week after the first oil well was struck in 1922. Because of all the people, it was a dangerous place to be after sundown. Mr. Pete was right. Even with the recent improvements made by the "boy mayor," Clyde Byrd, danger still plagued the town and its surroundings. He and Daniel couldn't wait to show their new friend around.

Abraham Lincoln Blackman was big for fifteen years old. He was already six feet tall, but it ran in his family. Just like Hank's daddy, Abraham's father was tall. When the colored boy smiled, his teeth shone bright against his rich, dark chocolate colored skin. When he first came to Farmville he looked scrawny, but he had filled out since eating Granny's cooking. The longer he worked for her the more defined his muscles became. He had the body of some of the adult men who worked in the oilfields, but he was still growing. Granny let him have a room in her barn. It was home to him.

Abraham's ma had lived in a tent at Beech Hill with his younger brothers and sisters during the summer, but she recently moved back across the river and south to be with family. She was never comfortable around the oil towns after the trouble with the Klan a couple of months back. So she left Abraham to make his own way with her blessing, and she returned to more familiar surroundings in northern Louisiana. Hank was glad Abraham stayed. He was his newest best friend and knew Daniel and Beth Ann felt the same way.

* * * * * * *

Daniel drove the Baker wagon for the first leg of the trip, passing the time by recounting the latest Sherlock Holmes story he'd read. This was the trip he and Hank had looked forward to all summer, but for some reason Hank was nervous. His senses were extraordinarily sharp all of a sudden. As they pulled onto the Smackover Road, Daniel's voice became a dull noise in the background. A dark dread pressed against Hank's chest, causing his pulse to race. Sweat formed in his armpits. When Mr. Pete looked back at them, the hairs on the back of Hank's neck rose and tingled. He felt compelled to search the woods on either side of the road.

Okay, this is weird. I definitely don't like it. Aren't the dreams enough, God? His stomach churned and the telltale pressure under his chin threatened to rob him of his breakfast. The feeling went away as fast as it came. Then, for several seconds, he had difficulty swallowing past his thickened tongue. He didn't want to alarm Daniel, so he closed his eyes and forced his mind to squash the panic smothering him. The battle took several minutes before his throat finally opened. His breathing was shallow, but he could breathe. *Daddy, what's happening to me?* He put his open palm on his friend's shoulder.

"Would you mind if I took a nap? I didn't sleep much last night."

"Go ahead." Daniel did a double take when he looked at Hank. "You don't look so good. Do you want me to get the deputy's attention?"

"No. I'm...just really tired. I'll be fine after I get some sleep."

Daniel nodded and slid to the middle of the bench while Hank slithered into the back of the wagon. He lay on his side, using his hands for a pillow against the wagon's floorboards and the bumpy ride. Fear pricked his nerves. He squeezed his eyes shut, barely keeping another wave of panic at bay. He couldn't shake the feeling that something bad was about to happen.

God, please keep all of us safe while we're in Smackover. And while you're at it, please protect Ma, Jimmy, and Granny, too.

The farther away from home they drove, the more intense the fear became. Unbidden tears fell from his eyes, rolling down his cheek and nose onto his hands. Anger took root and melted the terror from a moment ago. *Stop crying! You* never *cry. What would Daddy think if he could see you acting like a baby?* Without warning, every scene from yesterday morning's dream played out in crisp, vivid detail.

A strong voice reverberated clearly in Hank's ears. *Be strong. Have courage. I will never leave you. I'm always with you, right beside you, Hank. Trust your heart and not your eyes, son. Act wisely because there will be times you'll need to trust your eyes and not your heart.*

Hank squeezed his eyes shut. A sob shook his body. *I don't know what that means, and I don't want to know.* After several minutes, he lay on his back, exhausted. He repeated the prayer he shouted at God from his dream. *What do you want from me?*

After another couple of minutes, he sat up and crossed his legs, his palms flat against the cold bed of the wagon. He closed his eyes and recalled the events from the dream as if he were asleep: the voices under his window, Jimmy Jack's empty bed, chasing after the three men, and his inability to follow them into the woods. Then his eyes opened wide, and he became dizzy as the landscape around him spun out of control.

Huh! A fresh wave of nausea churned through his stomach. Shock and terror replaced the pity and anger of a few moments ago. He felt the familiar tingling spread from his neck to his scalp.

Jimmy Jack's bed was empty in my dream. Hank took a tumble and nearly bumped his head on the sideboard when the wagon pitched slightly on the uneven dirt road. He scrambled to brace himself with his back against the sideboard near the bench seat. His chest heaved as he rested his elbows on his trembling knees and wiped fresh tears with both hands. *He's in danger, isn't he, Daddy? "Like father, like son" could just as easily be you and Jimmy as it could be you and me or Abraham and his daddy.*

Silence.

This just keeps getting worse. He slumped back against the side of the wagon as despair threatened to overcome him. He thought about Jimmy's hero, the Golden Eagle. Then he thought about his own heroes: Daddy, Mr. Pete, Mr. Morgan, even Uncle Will.

What am I doing? This is stupid. I can't fall apart now. What happened to me proving I'm man enough to be treated like one, especially after this summer? This is embarrassing. Even my little brother has more guts than I do right now. What would Daddy say about that? He looked toward the other wagon. *What would Mr. Pete think about how I'm handling this whole situation?*

Hank dried his face on the sleeves of his duster. He sat up and looked at each of his three companions, and then he looked at the spreading clear blue of the morning sky overhead. The more he considered his heroes, the more resolved he was to regain his composure and take back control of his emotions and his choices.

Here's what you're going to do. Stop being a baby and do what Daddy or Mr. Pete would do to handle this. Think about how you handled yourself during the summer and do it again. Just stop being a whiner and get hold of yourself.

Indignation seeped into every pore of his body. All tension dissolved, and he allowed a quiet chuckle to cleanse his soul. *If I let fear dominate me with this, how will I ever convince Daniel his fear of Granny Rose is just crazy?*

In a flash, Hank's memory replayed the mysterious advice from the dream. *Hey, wait a minute!* He slapped his forehead. *The voice said I'm supposed to trust my heart instead of my eyes.* He stared at the back of Daniel's head. *I trust Daniel completely, Beth Ann, and Abraham, too. Maybe that's what it means. I've been going about this all wrong. Instead of trying to figure this out alone, I need to get help from the people I trust.*

Hank felt a huge weight lift from his shoulders and chest. His dark mood melted with the morning light. He looked into the brightening, cloudless sky overhead and closed his eyes as he breathed in the crisp air. A new strength from within warmed his body as a plan formed in his mind. He'd ask his friends to help him solve the mystery of the dream. But first, he had to focus on the task at hand.

He and Daniel had been looking forward to this trip for weeks. They were actually going to Smackover, for crying out loud. Granny needed winter supplies because a lot of her corn crop was destroyed by a fire back in July. Mr. Morgan's injuries from the razorback attack last month prevented him from going. So Mr. Pete volunteered to go as long as he, Daniel, and Abraham came along to help with the loading. While they were at it, they would get supplies for Ma, too. The excitement of seeing the "town God forgot" after dark in the daytime pushed away all other thoughts.

Hank took a long, deep breath and let it out slowly before implementing his new resolve. He looked around in awe and appreciation of nature's wonder, seeing the colors of fall as if for the first time. From the lay of the land on both sides of the road, he guessed they were more than halfway to the crossroads. He nearly took another tumble as he stood to climb back onto the seat beside his best friend. He used Daniel's shoulder to brace himself as he took his place beside him.

"Ahhh!" The mules skittered. Daniel nearly dropped the reins before grabbing them with his fists. Hank covered his friend's mouth with his palm then wiped it on his trousers. He sat hard onto the seat beside him and watched wide-eyed while Daniel struggled with the mules. His pulse raced until the animals were under control again. Both boys smiled and waved when the deputy and Abraham looked back at them briefly.

"Daniel, it was just me. Who else would it have been?" Hank unbuttoned his duster and fanned his face several times with the lapels. "Nice rein handling, by the way. You held on tight and kept them from flying all over the place. I'm impressed." He put his hands in his pockets after buttoning his coat again against the chilly morning air. Then a nervous giggle rumbled from deep in his gut when he saw Daniel's ghost-white face and wide-open eyes. He patted his friend's shoulder. "It's okay. Where was your mind?" He draped his forearms across his legs, relaxing in a slump while his own heart rate slowed from the excitement.

"I can't remember what I was thinking anymore, but my mind was definitely *not* on someone touching me from behind. You said you were going to sleep for a while. I didn't expect you to be back up here in ten, fifteen minutes. You scared me half to death and nearly caused a stampede in the process." He shook his head and let out a loud sigh. "You'd better be glad my hands were busy or you'd have been knocked to the ground. You'd have been in *real* trouble if I'd have fainted."

Without warning, Daniel's nervous giggle broke the tension of the moment. Hank joined him with a short spurt of spontaneous chuckles. Then both fell silent, almost at the same time, as if on cue.

"I was only back there for ten to fifteen minutes? Seriously?" Hank wrinkled his eyebrows as he considered the short time frame he'd spent grappling with his emotions. "I'm really sorry. I didn't mean to scare you like that." After several seconds, guffaws shook Hank till tears flowed.

"What?" Daniel's cheek twitched as a grin spread across his red face. "What's so funny now?"

Hank wiped the happy tears from his face. "You're the best friend for me, you know that? You have perfect timing for making me laugh when I need it most, want it or not." The deputy looked over his shoulder at them again and smiled as their chortles echoed off the trees. "Okay, my sides and cheeks really hurt now."

Hank massaged the sides of his mouth with the thumb and forefinger of one hand while grabbing the edge of the seat with the other as the wagon lurched once again. "That stupid dream has had me so worked up; I thought I was losing my mind until I saw your face just now. Thanks for the distraction."

"You're welcome…I think." They rode for about a mile without speaking, but spurts of laughter continued to lighten the mood as they approached the Cross Roads community and made the sharp turn toward Smackover.

Chapter 8

Daniel stood and wiggled his knees before sitting down again, maintaining control of the mules. "I guess we're not stopping. Do you want to take over driving anyway?"

"Nah, you go ahead. I'll take over for the ride home." Hank stretched and cradled the back of his head with his fingers interlocked together. He allowed the rhythmic clip-clop of the mules' hooves lull him into a moment's peace. Occasionally, the gentle pair of working farm animals snorted. Hank was surprised at how calming such sounds were on him after the chaos from a few minutes ago. Even the noise of the wagon wheels rattling as they rolled along the dirt road gave him a sense of serenity.

"So why do you think this dream is bothering you so much?"

Hank dropped his hands to his lap and slumped against the back of the bench. He sighed as he stretched his legs before propping both booted feet on the front panel of the wagon. Then he draped his arms across the backrest of the bench. "I'm not sure. I just know there's something different about this one."

"Maybe it's just a dream with no hidden meaning in it at all. Both my mom and grandma say you can have weird dreams and nightmares if you eat something right before going to bed without letting it digest. Grandma Jewel is a believer because *her* grandma swore it was true and proved it over and over. She also holds to the notion something out of the ordinary can happen during the day to bring them on. I don't understand it, but they believe it. Could that be why you had the dream?"

Hank pondered all the events from yesterday. "Not really, unless you count this trip. As best I can tell, everything that could have put any of those kinds of thoughts into my head happened *after* the dream." As he used both hands to rub the spot where his neck and shoulders joined, he realized his heart was calm for the first time since yesterday morning.

"You said your uncle wrote a letter to your ma. Maybe the letter triggered it."

"Again, not possible. Remember, I told you the deputy gave her the letter *after* the sheriff told us Uncle Will had been attacked and almost killed. It's just weird. I had this dream *before* we knew about *any* of this, unlike the other dream that seemed to explain what had already happened."

"Yeah, but do you think it happened *while* you were dreaming? I mean, it's possible the dream has something to do with preparing you for what had already happened, just like this summer, but without years of time between."

Hank grabbed the bench as the wagon rolled over an uneven patch in the road. "All I know for sure is it *feels* different." He blew out a frustrated sigh as he slumped back in his seat again, folding his arms across his chest. "It's hard to explain. The images are still crystal clear, and my senses were so sharp in the dream. It's like my mind is telling me every detail is important, like I'm *supposed* to remember all of it." He sighed again. "I think what bothers me the most is where this dream happens."

Daniel nodded. "Yeah."

"I didn't really know exactly where I was in the other dream, but *this* dream took place at home. I thought it was real the whole time."

"What with all the sheriff told you, you have to do something, especially if you're being warned before it becomes a living nightmare. What are you thinking?"

"Well, you, Beth Ann, and I make a really good team. Even Mr. Pete noticed it this summer. Our skills complement each other when we work together. That's our strength as friends and partners. I think that's the best approach. I just don't want to put either of you in harm's way."

"Don't worry about that. We're a team, and teams stick together. What about Abraham and the deputy?"

"I don't want to get Mr. Pete involved unless or until it's necessary, especially if there's nothing to worry about. As for Abraham, I don't want to assume he's with us. If he wants in, I'm all for it."

"I've noticed he's really good at reading people and situations. That's an important part of any investigation. I personally think he'll want in."

"We should be able to talk with him while we're in Smackover. Hopefully, Mr. Pete will let us look around by ourselves before loading up and heading home."

"Well, as an objective observer, I have some ideas if you're interested in hearing them."

Hank felt the tension in his head and shoulders ease and smiled. Watching Daniel put his inner Sherlock Holmes to work was always entertaining. "Go ahead, 'Mr. Holmes.' Tell me your thoughts."

"First, we need to determine whether there is a definite connection between what's happened with the escaped prisoners and the dream. Second, we need a plan if they are connected to get everything back to normal before anything bad happens.

Then we bring in our secret weapon when the time is right, thus preventing the dream from coming true."

"Secret weapon?"

"Yeah, Deputy Collins."

"How's he our secret weapon?"

"He's our link to law enforcement."

"That doesn't make him a secret weapon."

"It does if the bad guys don't know you're related to him. Of course, you're really not until after the wedding, but he's practically family already."

Hank giggled. "And you honestly wonder how you're related to your mom's side of the family?"

Daniel smiled. "What? I'm serious. My family's strangeness aside, it's a good plan. Until we know more, there's really not much else we can do."

Hank chuckled again before he sobered and shook his head a couple of times. "Yeah, you're right. Speaking of your family, as much as I hate to admit it, I *almost* believe there may be something to the bad things happening in threes. Last night I was thinking about all that's going on, and I can see a pattern. The only problem is how they line up. Some are related. Others aren't so clearly connected, like Mr. Morgan and his coming to the house last night acting really strange. It scared me, Daniel."

Hank relayed the encounter with their giant friend. He sat forward, his hands clasped tightly as his arms rested across his legs. "I don't understand what he could have meant, but I got the feeling it wasn't good. I don't know what bothers me more, his behavior or my reaction. I don't ever remember being so afraid, except maybe when I was in that cabin with the kidnappers. It's like fear is smothering me, and I don't know how to stop it."

Daniel fidgeted in his seat. "Surely you don't think Mr. Morgan has anything to do with your dream, do you? I don't see it. Give it some time. Something will happen to explain it all eventually.

We'll figure it out, but you're right. There is definitely at least one set of threes happening here. I shudder to think what Grandma would say if you were experiencing three *sets* of three bad events, one right after the other. She knows about these things, I'm telling you. It's spooky…okay, well, not the Granny Rose kind of spooky. That's something different altogether. But…"

Another fit of laughter threatened to start with Hank again. "You do know you are the only one in Frenchport who is convinced Granny Rose is evil or spooky or able to cast spells, don't you?"

Daniel just stared at him for several seconds, and then he turned his attention back to the road again. "Maybe everyone except me is unable to see her for what she really is because *you're* all under her spell. But I'd really rather not talk about her if you don't mind."

Hank's body shook as he snickered as quietly as he could. Daniel held the reins in one hand as he took his hat off to scratch his head then put it back on. "You know, the more I think on it, it's becoming clear everything you're dealing with has a definite connection to you specifically and this summer. Mr. Morgan's behavior might tie in, too. It's the power of three, I'm telling you. Grandma Jewel knows about these things."

All of a sudden, Hank became quiet as he considered Daniel's revelation. "I don't know, but there's something else from my dream that has me concerned. Do you remember me telling you Jimmy Jack's bed was empty when I got up to look outside the window?"

"Yeah…oh!" He glanced at Hank. "What do you think it means?"

"It's making me a little nervous because I don't know whether he's in danger or not. It was obvious his bed had been slept in, but where was he?"

"Don't you think he'd gone to the outhouse?"

Hank sat up, his forearms draped across his spread knees, his hands hanging loose. "I guess it's possible, but I don't think so. It was like the empty bed was significant. I was supposed to see it, but I don't know why. In the dream, whoever had been outside the window could have been in our room while I was asleep. There were three of them in all. When I called out to them, they ran away. One of them had something slung over his shoulder. I'm pretty sure it was Jimmy."

"Okay, I know I've encouraged this conversation, but can we change the subject for now? It's beginning to give me the willies, and now *I'm* getting that tingling feeling on the back of *my* neck."

"I know what you mean. Me, too." They looked at one another as they each rubbed the backs of their necks near the hairline. Hank smiled in spite of the nagging, eerie feeling creeping back from its subconscious slumber. "Let's not spoil this trip over all of this. We've been looking forward to going to Smackover since before school started."

"Yeah."

* * * * * * *

Hank was glad Daniel concentrated more on driving the mules for the next several miles than talking as they drew closer to the region known as Death Valley. It started at Peanut Hill and stopped at the railroad tracks separating it from the main street of Smackover. Deep ruts marked the road and made the drive trickier and the ride bumpier.

Try as he might, Hank couldn't keep his mind on having an enjoyable day. His thoughts jumped from the dream to the escaped prisoners to Uncle Will's attack. Then they went from Mr. Morgan's disturbing business with the family to the note Hank had chosen to keep to himself. But the eerie feeling he nursed while doing his chores and when in the house earlier puzzled him the most. He sighed.

What if it's all just a bunch of coincidences and I'm worrying over nothing? No, there's too much...

"We're getting close." Daniel's voice was soft, but loud enough to break Hank's train of thought. They had talked about having a healthy respect for the stretch of road before them. "This is Cooterneck. Peanut Hill is just ahead, and then the turn off toward Phillip's Camp. The creek is just beyond that. The railroad crossing is about a mile from there. I wonder if there's anything left of Mother King's place."

"I don't know. If you ask me, I think she's scarier than Granny Rose by a *whole* lot. Why are you so fascinated with her?"

"Actually, I can't stand her. I get angry every time I think about her. The preacher says we should pity her and pray for her, but I don't. The only way I know how to explain why I feel the way I do is because of her lack of a conscience. It's like I need to see for myself that she's really gone from the area for good. I was glad to hear her place burned."

"Wow." Hank was surprised by his friend's red-faced, passionate anger. He had never spoken so irate about anyone before, not even his cousin Cliff.

"Do you realize she has literally gotten away with the murder of those two college kids, maybe more? She's made a mockery of the law. Instead of justice being served, it's been tied up and left to die without the hope of her paying for her crimes. It's not right. She should be in jail, but she isn't because of her size. Her arrogance is holding our justice system hostage. She's free because she's so fat she won't fit through the doors of any jail cell, and I bet she did it on purpose. Don't get me started."

Hank had no intentions of getting him started...again. As they passed the charred sight of the U Auto Stop, his nerves tingled. The last mile into Smackover was by far the longest of the trip. It was as though the fingers of pure evil reached out to snatch and grab at them as they dared to trespass on its unholy ground. Hank was glad for the bright sun shining down on them.

* * * * * * *

Since the first oil well was struck, Smackover could not be described as a sleepy little town anymore. Businesses already showed signs of high volumes of activity, even on this early Saturday morning. Seven other wagons waited to be loaded in front of Granny's and the Bakers' wagons at the Ritchie Grocery

Company just across the railroad tracks heading south. Hank knew there would be plenty of time to show Abraham around before they needed to be back to help Mr. Pete load their supplies. They were anxious to get started, but they waited for the deputy's instructions.

While Deputy Collins placed their orders inside the busy store, the boys stayed on the covered porch, away from the flow of customers going in and out. They leaned against the railing as they watched the crowds go about their business across the way and down the street.

Daniel relayed the lore of the town when the street in front of them was nothing but a huge, bottomless mud puddle. Abraham listened wide-eyed to the stories about dead mules sinking completely out of sight in the mud after being cut loose from the others pulling heavy loads from the oilfield. According to Daniel's source, the locals swear mules aren't the only things buried under the pavement Mayor Byrd had put over the muddy gravel to give the road a hard surface. He pointed out the exact place where one incident happened, just a few yards from where they stood.

Abraham's smile slowly spread across his face. "Aw, now, don't be joshing me none. I may not be from around here, but I know when someone's trying to pull my leg."

Daniel's brows pointed almost straight up. "No, honest. I've seen the picture of a mule dead on the road right over there. I promise."

Hank chimed in. "Yep, I've seen that picture, too. I just don't know about the rest of what you said, but the part about a mule dying in the street is definitely true."

Just then, the deputy joined them on the porch. "All right, boys. Go on with your sightseeing plans. Make sure you have a good lunch because we'll need to be ready to load up at about one o'clock. We need to be back on the road home by two-thirty, if not before. Don't make me come looking for you. I want to get back before dark."

"How about we meet you at the American Café at noon, Mr. Pete? Since we won't be able to go to the picture show, we'll be able to show Abraham everything by then."

"Sounds good. I should be finished with my business by then, too. Stay out of trouble and enjoy yourselves."

Hank watched the deputy head south along the boardwalk to avoid a large mud puddle before crossing the road toward City Hall and Mayor Byrd's office. He blended into the crowd, and then he seemed to vanish into thin air. Just as Hank was about to jump from the porch of the Ritchie Grocery Company and follow Daniel and Abraham to the pool hall, his attention was drawn to a man crossing the street after leaving the Blue Moon Café next door. Hank only got a glimpse of the left side of the man's face as he watched him follow the exact path Mr. Pete just took. As recognition flooded his brain, everything moved in slow motion. He felt dizzy as an invisible telescope sharpened the familiar image of the man while all else around him blurred and went silent. Hank's brows came together in a scowl. "Uncle Will?"

Chapter 9

He's supposed to be in prison, hurt, practically dead. But how...? *He hasn't changed at all.* Anger compelled Hank to follow his uncle through the visual tunnel his mind had created. He put a mental bead on the man so he didn't lose sight of him in the crowd. He wanted to know why he had lied. Hank bounded down the steps onto the boardwalk, headlong into the smothering horde of oilfield workers.

The number of people milling Broadway in Smackover early on a Saturday morning challenged belief without experiencing it. Hank's ability to keep his mark in sight was severely limited. Before he stepped off the boardwalk to cross the muddy street, someone bumped into him, nearly knocking him off balance. In an instant, he lost sight of his uncle.

"Watch where you're going, boy."

No! "Uh...sorry...sir...." Panic filtered into Hank's mind as he tried to get back to the grocery and feed store. *I have to find him again. He needs to explain himself.* When he finally reached the porch steps again, he unbuttoned his coat as sweat soaked his armpits and collar. He stopped on the third step up, just high enough to view the crowd at eye-level to the men. He leaned his hip against the railing and shoved his hat away from his wet hairline. He wiped his forehead with his coat sleeve before setting his hat back in place. He had to use the brim to shield his eyes from the bright sunshine as the last of the early morning fog dissipated.

Thick vaporous clouds puffed around his face from his ragged breathing. He realized the lack of common sense to his actions as he searched the faces all around him, but it didn't keep him from looking. The panorama showed only a host of strangers. *He was crossing the street, like he was following Mr. Pete. I know it was him, but…*

Just then, someone laid a heavy hand on his shoulder. He jerked his head around to identify the person touching him. Every nerve tingled from his face and head to his neck and shoulders. Hank let out a long, heavy sigh of relief when he realized his friends stood by him. *Why is this happening to me?* "Abraham…Daniel… you scared me half to death."

"What's going on with you? Abraham and I thought you were right behind us. When we realized you weren't, we saw you go in a completely different direction and then come back over here. We've been trying to get your attention. Aren't you coming with us?"

"Uh…well, I…" He scratched the back of his neck under his hat, looking back and forth between his friends and the crowd on Broadway.

"Uh-oh, I know that look."

"I had to get back to the porch, guys. I have to find him."

"Okay, come on, Abraham. This is no time to leave him alone, believe me. Let's get higher, Hank, so we can see over all these people." The three boys pushed against the flow of people leaving the Ritchie Grocery Company, back to the corner of the porch they'd left a few minutes earlier. When they reached the spot, Daniel put his hands on Hank's shoulders. "Now, talk to us.

Something has you all riled up. You obviously saw someone you didn't expect to see. Who are you looking for? We'll help you."

Hank turned back toward the street. Tears threatened to spill over his cheeks as he searched the myriad of unfamiliar faces. He wiped his eyes and allowed hot anger to replace his frustration and panic. He slapped the rail.

"I've lost him."

Then he turned toward his friends, nostrils flaring, jaw clenched, and mouth set in a tight line.

The worry lines on Abraham's forehead deepened. Hank heard the conversation between his friends, but he didn't acknowledge it. "What's got him so upset? He's practically wild. Have you ever seen him like this before?"

"Yeah, he's like this when his mind is set on something serious. He's trying to decide what to do next. You should have seen him when he took on the Klan out at Beech Hill when you were in trouble. He had this same look on his face before he took off and lit into them. The way he's acting, I'd say whoever he saw is a threat of some kind."

Hank turned his focus back on the crowd, his knuckles white and his face red as he grasped the railing. "I need to find him, Daniel, before..."

"Oh, boy...this is bad...really bad, Abraham. He's scared *and* angry. I can only think of one person he'd be so worried about right now."

Daniel grabbed hold of Hank's upper arms and turned him so his back was to the street. "Don't even think of doing anything alone. We're with you, but you need to help us understand. You're barely making sense. Are you looking for the deputy? He went to City Hall, remember? Is he in danger?"

Hank struggled to leave, but Daniel's hold was strong. "I've got to go, before he gets away."

"We'll find him, but who are you looking for? I'm not letting you go till you...oh, wait.... Are you looking for the man who kidnapped you, the escaped prisoner? He's here in Smackover? Come on, Hank, let us help you. What does he look like?"

Hank relaxed his body. "Uncle Will..."

Daniel let go of his friend's arms and put his fists on his hips. He took a step back, his brows furrowed. "Uncle Will? The escaped prisoner looks like your Uncle Will?"

"Yeah...I mean, no..."

"Okay, I'm really confused. Back up and start at the beginning. What happened?"

Hank looked from Daniel to Abraham, finally realizing how they must be reading his actions. *All right, that's enough. Stop behaving like this before you lose your mind and your friends because of stupid choices.*

He took a more relaxed stance, bracing himself against the porch rail with his hands and backside. He hoped his friends could tell he had calmed down, even though he was still shaking on the inside.

He drew in a deep breath and released it before speaking. "I saw Uncle Will cross the street a few minutes ago. He was leaving the Blue Moon when I first noticed him. I think he was following Mr. Pete. At least, it looked that way. And he was in a hurry."

"But I thought he was in Texarkana, in prison and badly hurt."

"Yeah, me, too. That's what the sheriff told us yesterday. To tell you the truth, I don't know what to think right now, but I know what I saw."

"Then how...? Oh, boy...this can't be good. So what do you want to do?"

Hank's shoulders slumped as he turned to face the busy thoroughfare before them, his arms akimbo. He mentally ran through his options and let several seconds pass before he shared his decision. "You guys go on without me. I need to find Mr.

Pete. He needs to know what I saw. It's already getting on mid-morning, and I don't want to waste our fun time on something I can't control or do anything about. Go ahead and show Abraham around like we'd planned. I'll catch up with you as soon as I can."

"Are you're sure?"

Hank put his hands in his coat pockets and nodded. He smiled as he willed peace to wash over him. Then he turned back to face his loyal friends, resolving to enjoy this trip and keep a lighthearted tone to his words. "Yeah, go on and get that Coca Cola you've been talking about all week. I won't be long. I hope not, anyway. I'll look for you at the soda fountains, even if I have to go to all the drug stores to find you."

"Okay, just be careful going off by yourself."

Hank's conscience fought to stay calm as thoughts of his discovery threatened to reverse his resolve of a few moments ago. "I'll be okay. Uncle Will just makes me so mad I can hardly see straight sometimes. Why would he lie to us, Daniel, especially to Ma? All he does is hurt her while all she does is love him. He's up to something. I intend to find out what, but not today. We're here to have some fun. Sorry I almost ruined it for us."

Daniel's face finally relaxed. "Yeah, I understand what you mean about your uncle. Try not to let it upset you too much…today, anyway…and till you get some answers. We're with you, just like Beth Ann told you yesterday. Let's work together on this as a team."

"He's right, you know." Abraham placed his warm, dark hand on Hank's shoulder. "You shouldn't deal with this alone. Look, you're more than friends to me. You're my family. I care, and I want to be your partner in this with Daniel and Beth Ann. I understand what you feel, more than you know. Go ahead and tell Deputy Collins what you saw, and then find us and let's put all this behind us while we're here. Don't borrow from tomorrow what you can't do anything about today. I'm not saying forget about it, just set it aside till you can think more clearly and make the right decisions for what to do next."

Hank allowed a new strength to flow through him as Abraham's gentle voice pierced through the emotions he had allowed to take over his sound judgment. "How'd you get to be so wise, Abraham? You know, as far as we're all concerned, you *are* a member of our team. We just need you to speak your mind more often. Add your thoughts and ideas to the discussions. I respect your opinions. I have since the first day we met. You're a good friend. Thanks for helping me find the right perspective on all of this."

"You're welcome."

Daniel cleared his throat with a lot more noise than normal. "Well, are we done being serious for a while, because I definitely need a Coca Cola to wet my mouth and throat. I can't even spit right now."

Hank grinned, allowing his closest friend to dislodge the tension choking him. He didn't want to ruin their plans to enjoy their time in Smackover any more than he already had. Now was not the time to deal with these things. He definitely needed a more level-headed approach to this new development. He took a quick, deep breath, glad to be thinking more clearly. "Sure. Get out of here. I'll catch up with you after I find Mr. Pete. I promised to let him know if I saw or heard anything related to what the sheriff told us yesterday."

Abraham rubbed his hands together, his face glowing and his eyes bright as a wide grin spread across his face. His white teeth contrasted sharply against the dark brown color of his skin. "All right, that's a good plan. Come on, Daniel. I'm thirsty too, but I think I'll pass on a Coca Cola, though. My mouth's been watering for an RC Cola since we hit town. That and a Moon Pie. I haven't had an RC and a chocolate Moon Pie since I left home. It's time I took care of that here and now."

Hank watched his friends blend into the crowd as they made their way to the Murphy Building. He took another deep breath and then let it out slowly before he took the same path to City Hall he'd watched the deputy and Uncle Will take. As he entered the narrow alley between the Turner Store and the theater, Hank immediately noticed the noise on the street took on a quiet, hollow sound. That along with an eerie darkness put him on edge. *Don't give in to your imagination. It's just the early morning shadows.* He stopped in his tracks when a chill shook his body. *Oh, no, not again. Come on, God. Give me a break, okay?*

Blood raced through his throbbing veins as he recognized the noise of a riot spilling into the alley from the small, barred windows of the over-crowded jail. *Don't borrow trouble. Find Mr. Pete then get on with the day we've planned.* He forced himself to walk with a steady pace as he made a beeline for the door to City Hall.

The stench of discarded food and body odor assaulted his nostrils till he held his breath. About thirty feet from his intended destination, he had just taken another quick breath to hold when a large hand clamped over his mouth. Hank flailed his arms and legs at his captor's head and body, pummeling, scratching, and kicking with all his might.

The mystery man put his thick-muscled, free arm around Hank's chest, lifting him off the ground and quickly carrying him through the alley to the back of the theater. Hank tried to yell out as he grabbed the man's shirt collar and pulled on a chain around his neck till it broke. The man tightened his hold before lowering Hank to the ground unceremoniously, staying in the shadows and close to the building.

"Hold still and be quiet, you hear, Hank? I really don't want to hurt you."

Hank's heart hammered against his chest as his mind realized the man called him by name. *I did see him...Uncle Will.* He nodded and stopped fighting, even though breathing was difficult through his partially covered nostrils. The man loosened his hold around Hank's chest, but continued to restrain him and keep his mouth covered

"I thought that was you following me. I really wish you hadn't seen me. This complicates things more than you can imagine, for you as well as for me. You really are your father's son, aren't you? He had a way of making things difficult, too. Don't let your curiosity get the better of you. You need to stay out of this. There's a lot more going on than you know. You have no idea who you've messed with and what he's capable of."

Hank recognized anger in the words from the uncle he knew so well, but there was something else he couldn't quite identify. As he half listened, his brain instantly flashed through the events from the day before. *The note! Wait, what did he just say? I thought...he thinks I was following him? But I lost him. If not me, then who...?* Hank closed his eyes as he realized a black cloud hovered on the fringes of his consciousness, moving slowly inward, engulfing him in its wake. *Don't pass out. I can't pass out. God, help me not pass out, please.*

As his arms began to go limp, he realized his left fist tightly held something hard. The sudden revelation chased away the darkness. *Hide it. Don't let him know you have it.* Hank put the object into his coat pocket without drawing attention to the move, he hoped. As he shifted his posture to do so, breathing became easier.

"Now...I'm going to take my hand away from your mouth. Do you promise not to yell out?"

Hank nodded.

"Okay, but don't turn around, either. Understand?"

Hank nodded again. *When he lets go, run!*

"Good." Uncle Will moved his hand away from Hank's mouth.

Before he could run away, both of his shoulders were weighed down by the man's hot hands. *Doggone it. Of course, he'd know what I was thinking. He's Uncle Will. We used to be so close, like brothers, but now...*

"I'm only going to say this once. So listen carefully. We have eyes and ears all around. You can't stop us, so don't be a hero. You won't like the consequences. Be careful what you say and who you talk to. We're watching and listening, and we won't let you ruin things for us this time. We know where you live, and we know who your friends are."

The more Hank heard, the less sure he was about being able to stand on his own if he were released right then. His knees shook and his muscles were in knots.

"Before I let you go, I want you to promise to look straight ahead and count to a hundred. Then you'll be free to go on about your business. Got it?"

Hank nodded, afraid to speak. Without warning, he was pushed to the ground. He broke his fall with his hands, but not before the side of his face hit the gravel. He was sure his cheek, nose, and forehead were bleeding, maybe his ear, too.

"Don't get up till you're through counting. I'll know if you cheat."

Chapter 10

Hank waited several minutes before moving, more concerned about how to explain his injuries than counting. As he sat up, he dusted himself off and checked his hands and face. Thin broken lines of blood streaked both palms, but he winced at the cuts on his nose, cheek, and ear, the bleeding being more significant. He hoped the bump on his forehead looked smaller than it felt. He was sure it already showed signs of bruising.

This is messed up. Who does he think he is threatening us, his own family, and my friends? What's wrong with him? This is far worse than I ever expected things to be between us. It's like I don't know him at all. He certainly doesn't know me if he thinks I'm just going to give up without a fight. Because he's definitely right about one thing, I am my father's son.

Just then, he heard the door to City Hall open. Before it closed, he heard voices. He peeked around the corner and saw Mr. Pete and Mayor Byrd shake hands as they talked. Hank quickly scooted against the back wall of the theater, not ready for anyone to see him yet. Unsure of which voice was whose, he heard one of the men say he'd keep the other informed about something indistinguishable. Shouts from another riot in the jail erupted, making it difficult to focus on the conversation.

Once it was quiet again in the alley, Hank relaxed. *I need to get out of here.* He looked around him. *Amazing! Broadway is so full of people, but there's no one back here. I guess the jail keeps everyone away from this part of town.* Then he looked across the way where a lynch mob had strung up a colored man not long ago. *This isn't the best place to be for any length of time, day or night. I need to get out of here.*

As he tested his ability to stand without falling, he remembered the object he had hidden in his coat pocket. He leaned against the wall as he put a shaky hand into his left pocket and pulled out a plain, silver-colored chain of tiny balls linked together except where it was irreparably detached. He transferred it to his right hand and checked the pocket for anything else, but found nothing.

Just a chain? Uh-uh, it's not a piece of jewelry. He looked around on the ground before he returned it to his coat pocket and dropped to both knees, sliding his hands through the dirt and grass. *Something was on that chain. Something important, or else why wear it? What would he have put on it?*

After searching for a couple of minutes where they had stood, Hank sat back on his heels. *Think...where were you when you grabbed it off his neck?* He replayed the entire incident in his mind, and then his gaze followed the narrow space between the buildings, toward Broadway. *Yeah...I was coming this way from over there when he picked me up and brought me back here. Look in the alley.*

Hank crawled around on the ground, carefully running his hands over the dry dirt and sprigs of grass growing near the building across from City Hall. He followed the same path they had used to get to the back of the theater. Just as he was about to give up, he saw something metallic in the dirt and partially hidden in a tuft of grass. It was about ten feet from the end of the alley where he had been taken. *What's this? Could it be...?* He looked in both directions and behind him before he picked up the object.

"It's a key." He didn't realize he'd spoken. *This is it…this is what was on the chain. I'd bet my life on it.* He turned it over several times, studying it. *It's not a door key. I wonder what it opens.*

Movement behind the theater startled Hank, so he put the key in his pocket with the chain. He grunted as he stood, feeling the pain from the fall in every muscle, it seemed. Since Mr. Pete was no longer at the mayor's office, there was no reason to go there now. So he decided to catch up with Abraham and Daniel.

* * * * * * *

Hank found his friends sitting outside of Fagg's Blacksmith and Mechanic Shop. Abraham sat with his elbows on his legs, his hands clasped, and his face the epitome of gloom and doom. Daniel sat beside him, his mouth pressed in a thin line, his nostrils flaring, and his chest heaving with every breath. *Looks like I'm not the only one who had a run-in with trouble.*

From the redness of Daniel's face and neck, Hank knew his friend was fired-up angry. *Uh, oh!* He recognized righteous indignation when Daniel pounded one of his fists into the other hand and ground it like it was a baseball. Hank noticed his white knuckles from a couple of stores away, and waited till he was in front of Berry's Drug Store to speak. The stinging cuts on the side of his face throbbed as he wiped his sweaty palms on his duster. *Well, here goes…okay…just act normal. Maybe they won't notice anything.*

"Hey, guys. What's wrong? I thought you were going to get a soda."

Daniel shook his head and spoke without making eye contact. "Don't get me started unless you're ready to…." He looked up, and his face immediately changed from red hot anger to dropped-jaw, wide-eyed puzzlement. His fists relaxed, but he stayed seated. "What happened to you? You look like you've been in a fight."

Abraham stood, flexing his fists at his sides, and his furrowed brows accented the flash of anger Hank saw momentarily in his eyes. He hadn't seen that kind of reaction from their gentle friend since his ma had been in danger at Beech Hill back in July.

Hank sat down. *Oh, boy. They noticed.* "I'm all right. Both of you relax. I…I fell, okay? It's nothing, really, but I take it you can't say the same?"

Daniel continued to stare at Hank's face. His voice was soft, clearly distracted by what he saw. "We, uh…we sat down at the counter to order our sodas at the pool hall. Then um…they um… they said Abraham had to leave, that his money was no good there. You know you're bleeding, don't you?"

"Yeah, I do, but it's nothing." Hank took a handkerchief from the back pocket of his pants and dabbed at his wounds. He wondered why he hadn't thought to do so before now. "So that's it? That's why you're spitting mad?" His friend just stared and nodded, clearly dumbfounded. "Well, that makes two of us."

As Hank put his handkerchief back in his pocket, he shook his head. "I'm so sorry, Abraham. I just don't understand people like that. My daddy always taught me to judge a man by his character, not his color or appearance. Why can't everyone else do the same? It's just wrong how you're treated. I hate how your people are put down by those who think they're better than anybody else. Especially when it's obvious they're so far beneath *you* in character. It's not fair. They act so superior when they aren't."

"Don't worry about it, Hank. My mammy and pappy taught me to just let it go. I live by their example, but I'm no saint, believe me. It's hard to ignore sometimes, but they always said I needed to *choose* to not let it bother me. They told me if I didn't, I'd be no different or better than those who judged me for what I am instead of who I am."

"It's still wrong. It embarrasses me, how they enjoy making you feel like the dirt under their feet."

Abraham looked over at Hank and smiled. "Don't be embarrassed for me. They only succeed when I choose to let them."

Daniel stood abruptly and faced the other two, causing Hank's heart to jolt. "Hey, I have an idea. Abraham, how much money do you have? I'm not trying to pry. I just have an idea for getting our sodas and your moon pie that'll serve those guys right for being so uppity. What they don't know won't hurt them...or me. But it'll sure make me feel better."

Abraham pulled his money from his pocket. "I've got nearly three dollars in change. What are you thinking about doing?"

"Give me a dollar." Daniel took a dollar bill from his own pocket and swapped it for Abraham's change. "I'm going to use *your* money to buy our sodas and your moon pie. I'll have to get the sodas in bottles, if that's okay. It's not the same as when they come from the fountain, but they're still good. I'll show them your money *is* just as good as mine, but they'll *think* it's mine. Do you want anything, Hank?"

Hank looked over at Abraham, chuckling. "Yeah, get me a Pepsi Cola and a moon pie." He took two bits from his pocket and gave it to Daniel.

Abraham's smile brightened the mood. "See? My mammy and pappy were right. When you choose to *not* let bigoted people bother you, you'll find ways to turn it around on them." The colored boy smacked his lips. "My mouth's watering already."

Daniel grinned. "Good. Now, this is what I call having fun, but don't think you're going to get away without telling us about that fight, Hank. I'll be right back."

"But...I fell...." Hank sighed, shaking his head. "What's the use? He's in his own little world right now, not listening to a single word we're saying."

As Daniel ran down the boardwalk toward the pool hall in the Murphy Building, Hank sat back, leaning against the building, and let out a long sigh. Abraham's voice had a hint of worry in it when he spoke. "You're not a good liar, I hope you know."

Hank looked over at his colored friend and swallowed, his face heating up. "What do you mean?"

"You're worried about something. It's all over your face, and I don't mean the cuts and bruise. Did you find your uncle? Did he do that to you?"

Hank let a puff of air escape his lips. *Daniel's right. Abraham is good at reading people.* He dabbed his wounds with his handkerchief again. "It's complicated, but…I'd better wait for Daniel to try to explain it. I have to be careful, but I trust you guys. Suffice it to say I'm being watched, it seems. So…"

Just then, he noticed Daniel walking toward them with his arms full of their snacks. "Wow! That didn't take long." Hank smiled as a grin spread wide across Daniel's face. His eyes had the familiar sparkle of mischief Hank knew all too well. As their friend reached the drug store next door to the old livery-turned-garage, he and Abraham stood.

"Boy did that feel good. You should have seen that soda jerk's face when I asked him if my money was good for three sodas and a couple of moon pies. From his expression, he must have thought I was a loony or something. He asked if I had been dropped on my head. I told him no, but that I wanted to make sure my money was good after he told that other fellow his wasn't." Daniel handed out sodas and moon pies and giggled. "It was great. He was completely clueless. What a numbskull!"

"I have a question for you. Why didn't you and Abraham just go to another place to get your sodas?"

"Hank, are you kidding me? Think about it! It was a matter of principle. Besides, they made me mad. You know how I get when that happens. It's a good thing Abraham kept a level head about it. I was ready to jump those guys and beat the living daylights out of them. I wasn't in any kind of respectable attitude to go anywhere else. So we sat down here and you came along not long afterwards. Now, enough about me, I want to know what happened to you."

Hank tried to be inconspicuous as he checked out the men loitering around open shop doors, searching for Uncle Will among them. *Whoa! Wait a minute! Uncle Will said "we" have eyes and ears everywhere. Who was he talking about?* His heartbeat hammered against his chest as he realized he didn't know who could be spying on him.

"Not now, not here. Let's go over there to the church porch, away from the crowds around the shops."

The boys crossed the street to the Methodist church steps. As they indulged in their snacks and sodas, Hank relaxed and enjoyed the company of his friends, especially Daniel. He made them laugh when he belched, one in particular sounded like a bullfrog. It felt good to laugh, although it hurt because his body was sore from the shove Uncle Will had given him earlier. At one point he laughed so hard he had to wipe tears from his eyes. He couldn't help snickering every so often for several minutes afterwards. When they were all out of soda, Daniel returned the bottles to the pool hall.

Abraham reclined on the steps, his elbows propping him up. "I can see why you and Daniel are such good friends. He's something else, isn't he?"

Hank mimicked Abraham's repose. "Yeah, he is. He's like a brother to me. You know we were born just minutes apart, don't you?"

"Oh, yeah, you did mention that before." He grinned. "It actually explains a lot."

Hank chuckled. "Yeah, my ma says it's like we're twins, but born to different parents, whatever that means."

Abraham nodded. "I can see it. I don't know how I could have forgotten. You two think so much alike you know each other's thoughts, almost without having to say anything. You're definitely connected. Some people would find what you two share spooky."

"Do me a favor, and don't tell Daniel that."

Abraham chuckled. "Yeah, he's a bit skittish about things he can't explain."

"It's interesting how he can be so unafraid of what is obviously dangerous, but spooky stuff gives him the willies. I trust him though, you know?"

"Yeah, I do. It's important to have someone you can rely on for anything. Believe me, there's nothing lonelier than not having someone you can tell anything to, no matter what it is. Until I met you, that was me. I had no one. I'm glad we're friends, Hank. I really am. You, Daniel, and Beth Ann are different from everyone else. So are Granny Rose, Deputy Collins, and your mammy."

Hank felt heat rise from his neck to his face. "We're, what Ma would say, blessed to know you, Abraham. I'm glad you stayed when your ma left for Louisiana."

"It was time I made my own way. She has enough to worry about now that Pappy is gone. She knows I'm in a good place where people care about me. I'm glad I stayed, too."

"Hey, you're not getting serious again, are you?" Daniel joined them on the steps and struck the same pose as Hank and Abraham.

"No, I was just telling Abraham how glad we are he stayed when his ma left."

"I'll say. I was beginning to think no one wanted to come to Farmville, much less live there. After all, it's not exactly in the middle of the boom towns and all, but it's not a bad place to live, either. By the way, how is your ma? Is she settling in okay where she went in Louisiana?"

"I guess she's doing fine. I haven't really heard anything, but I take that as being good. If something were wrong, I think I'd know. So I consider no news as good news. Besides, she's with family. They'll take good care of her."

Daniel nodded. "That's good. Does your family come from Louisiana?"

"Well, not exactly. We actually came to America, to Virginia, from the west coast of Africa."

Hank shifted his body to keep the pain from showing on his face. "So you have family members who were slaves?"

Abraham nodded. "Yeah, but they weren't like most slaves. You see, they had a really caring owner who allowed them to earn wages to buy their freedom. He helped them learn trades and bought whole families so he could keep them together."

Daniel's eyebrows pointed toward his hairline. "Wow! I didn't think that was allowed. You hear so many stories about families being split up."

"Yeah, my family's owners bought them before they were put on the auction blocks. He had to pay the trader a lot more to be able to do his business privately."

Hank stretched his legs out and crossed them at the ankles. "How did he know who were families?"

"I don't really know, but my great-grandfather was the chief of our tribe. Maybe he and his family carried themselves differently. All I know is they were bought by this man, and they had a very special relationship with him. Whenever a new ship came into the harbor, my great-grandfather went with him to point out more families from our tribe when he had room for more. The relationship between owner and slave became a bond of trust and respect for one another. While my great-grandfather learned to speak English, he taught his owner-friend his African language. It helped him when he went to the slave trader because he was able to secretly communicate with the new arrivals from our tribe."

Daniel's brows came together in a scowl. "How did your great-grandfather and his family end up on a slave ship in the first place?"

Abraham shifted his seating position before stretching his own legs out. "An enemy tribe overthrew them in the night and sold them to the white slave traders."

Daniel shook his head. "Wow, that's not what I expected you to say at all. What was the man's name who bought your family?"

Abraham smiled. "Mr. Abraham Paul White was his name. I haven't thought about him in a long time."

Hank looked at their friend. "So why didn't your family take his last name when Mr. Lincoln freed the slaves?"

"Mr. White told my great-grandfather and his family it was important to maintain their integrity in spite of their circumstances because it's what shapes character. He also told them to never be ashamed of who they were because it defined them. So when they were freed, they decided to take 'Blackman' as their surname in honor of their skin tone. It was as much a statement of who they were as their integrity and character."

"I like that, Abraham, don't you, Daniel?"

"Yeah."

Abraham smiled, and then frowned, his attention on someone on the street in front of the church. He slowly stood, his fists clenched by his sides.

Hank grabbed a fistful of his friend's coattail. "Whoa! Where are you going?"

Chapter 11

Abraham shook away from Hank's grasp and took long strides as he walked south on Broadway, away from town. Hank let his friend go without protest when he noticed five armed riders on horseback watching them. They sat with their rifle and shotgun barrels pointed up with the stocks of their weapons resting on their thighs. *Vigilantes!* Hank's heart flashed with palpitations.

"Come on, Daniel, something's wrong. It's not safe for him to go off alone." Hank nodded in the direction of the men. "Those guys might be wearing badges, but they don't represent the law like Mr. Pete and Sheriff Stan do." They scrambled to catch up with Abraham.

"Why is he in such a hurry?" Daniel looked behind them.

"Don't look back. They might wonder what *we're* up to and come this way. I've heard stories about them you really don't want me to repeat. They may not lynch us, but they'll shoot first and then ask questions, *if* we're still alive."

As they entered the residential area, Hank reached out and touched Daniel's shoulder. "Okay, hold up. Let's stop, but make it look like we were racing or playing tag." They stopped in the middle of the street. "We should laugh or something." They grinned as their chests heaved, resting their hands on their hips.

Daniel took off his hat and wiped his brow with his sleeve before putting it back on his head. "You know, I'm getting the feeling this trip has been jinxed, but I'm trying really hard not to think too much about that because…well, you know."

"Yeah, what were we thinking? Having *fun* in Smackover? This town's shady reputation isn't any better in the daytime if you ask me." Hank looked around and sighed when he saw the men ride off in the opposite direction. "Good—they're going toward the railroad—but we still need to find Abraham. Do you see him?"

Daniel nodded toward a nearby house. "Yeah, he's over there, slowing down and…huh, looking at someone's yard full of drying laundry? Strange." He shook his head. "It's not like he's never seen clothes hanging on a line before."

Hank checked behind them again before nudging his partner in the direction of the fenced yard. "Come on, let's go. Just be careful. We don't need to draw attention to ourselves." They jogged to join their friend where he had stopped.

Abraham stood with his back to them, his fists clenched at his sides. The fence surrounding the yard looked like a corral. Clothes billowed in the light, morning breeze.

Hank glimpsed a tall, lanky, blond-haired boy go inside the house before the screen door slammed shut with a distinct pop.

Daniel gasped. "Wasn't that…?"

Hank was sure they shared the same thought. "I'm not sure. But let's not jump to conclusions before we know what's going on here." He stepped up alongside Abraham and draped his forearms on the top rail of the fence between the street and yard. He rested a booted foot on the bottom rail. "What's so interesting about this yard, Abraham? Do you know the kid who went in the house just now?"

"No, but I know the shirt he was wearing. I recognize some of those clothes hanging over there, too." Abraham used his chin to point to the clotheslines.

Hank noticed their friend grab the top log of the fence with shaky hands. "Whose are they?" He watched the colored boy's eyes pool with unshed tears.

"They're my pappy's." The big boy wiped his face with his shirtsleeves without letting go of his grip, and then he sniffled. "I'd know his shirts anywhere."

Daniel drew in a quick breath and copied Hank's stance as he flanked their friend. "How'd you know to come here?"

Before he spoke, the colored boy cleared his throat. "I saw a kid…he looked to be about my age. He was…." There was a slight tremor in his voice. His lips quivered as his brows furrowed deeply. "He was *wearing* my *pappy's favorite* shirt. I followed him here." A sob shook his body briefly, tears streaming down his face. Then he coughed and took a deep breath, standing tall for a few seconds before his shoulders slouched. He wiped the fresh tears from his cheeks, using his shirtsleeves.

Hank swallowed, making eye contact with Daniel, and then he focused on Abraham's face. "You're absolutely sure of what you saw?"

Abraham nodded as another tear dripped from his lashes and rolled down his cheek. "No doubt whatsoever. What do you suppose it means?"

"I don't know, but before we go knocking on the door and confronting anyone, tell *us* how you know the shirt the stranger wore belonged to your pa."

Their friend looked down then back up, staring in the direction of the drying clothes. "When Mammy made it, she used the tribal colors of our ancestors in Africa. Did you see the striped shirt that yellow-haired boy wore?"

"I really didn't pay much attention to what he wore. Describe it to us."

Abraham crossed his arms over the top of the fence. "The colors are black, red, green, and gold—not yellow, but gold. The sleeves are black. The stripes framing the sleeves and along the sides are red. Those colors distinguish our tribe from others in the region. Green stripes are next. They are narrower because they represent our family. The color over the chest and back looks like gold armor, the symbol of the tribal chief."

Daniel shifted his position as he switched feet on the bottom rail. "Hey, you're talking about your family crest, kind of."

Hank nodded. "Yeah, but that may not be enough to convince these people it belongs to you, or the other clothes you recognize on the lines over there."

"Actually, there's more. Mammy sewed a set of emblems under the buttons that no one would think to look for. You remember the four-leaf clover I showed you under the collar of the shirt you found on the skeleton this summer?"

Hank draped his arms across the top rail, resting his chin on them. "Yeah, I do."

"There are more that I didn't show you, under the buttons, and they tell our story. They're on all his shirts. It's our family's custom, and one of his shirts would have been passed down to me when I married. Then Mammy would teach my wife how to preserve our heritage so our story never died. I thought they were lost forever with Pappy being dead and all."

Hank looked at the clotheslines on the other side of the fence. "Why didn't you tell us about the other emblems before now?"

"Pappy always told me to treat our story with respect and honor, not pride. To him, it was more important for us to be who we were by our actions than flaunt it with emblems that were meaningless without the proof." Abraham grinned as his chin quivered. "He said the one who let pride carry him away with self-importance was like the peacock, all noise and color on the outside and no real beauty from the inside."

"So how many emblems are you talking about?"

"There are five. They go from bottom to top. The first one is a set of shackles. The second is a cross. The third is a dove. The fourth is a fish, and the last one is the sun."

"What do they represent, if you don't mind me asking?"

Abraham smiled as he shook his head and took a deep breath. "The shackles represent our slave heritage. The cross represents the freedom we have now. The dove represents the peace that fills us from the inside out. The fish represents the guidance we are given to live with integrity. The sun represents the light of our future."

Daniel gripped the top fence rail and hefted himself onto the next to the bottom rail. "We have to get those shirts back for him, Hank. I wouldn't want a stranger wearing my family crest. It's a matter of honor. They're too important for just anyone to wear."

"I agree, but how do we..."

"I appreciate the thought, Daniel, but this is something I need to do myself. I just need to look under one button." Without warning, Abraham climbed the rails and jumped into the yard.

Daniel followed behind him. "Come on, Hank."

Just then, the noise of a screen door slamming shut reverberated inside Hank's head. He tried to get over the fence, but his feet would not lift off the ground. His legs wouldn't work, either. "Wait...I can't...." *Someone's coming. I've got to get to them so they're...* Adrenaline pumped through his veins as he willed his muscles to propel him into action and follow his friends. He barely caught up to them when he heard someone pump a shotgun close by. He saw the gun barrel before he saw who carried it come around the clothes on the line between them and the house.

"Stealing is a serious crime around these parts, no matter what you take. It doesn't matter if you hang or I shoot you. I still won't lose any sleep over the death of thieves."

Daniel gasped, his mouth and eyes wide open. "I knew it. Charlie Hutch!"

Hank threw his hands up at ear level. "Whoa! Charlie, stop. Put that thing down before someone gets hurt. We're not thieves." He slowly lowered his hands, wiping his palms on his pants legs before hooking his thumbs in his belt loops. "I'm Hank…Hank Baker… from Farmville, and this is Daniel. Don't you remember us? This here is our friend Abraham. His family lived out at Beech Hill when we met you in July. We're not stealing anything. We're just looking."

Charlie's brows came together in a scowl as he looked from Hank to the others, keeping the shotgun leveled on them. "Just looking for what? There's nothing here that belongs to any of you. You just need to leave. You're trespassing on private property."

Hank stepped forward, away from the other two. "You live here? How long have you been in Smackover? We looked for you all around Snow Hill. We wanted to find out how you and your ma were doing, but no one would tell us where you were."

"We couldn't stay there, not after what Floyd and my father had done. Everyone treated me and Ma like we had the plague."

"I'm sorry, Charlie. You didn't deserve that kind of treatment. You didn't do anything wrong. You're not responsible for what your brother and pa did. As far as I'm concerned, you were one of the good guys then, and you are now, too. How about putting that shotgun down, and let's all be friends here."

"What makes you so sure I'm one of the good guys, much less want to be your friend?"

"Because when you saved those people at Beech Hill, you did the right thing. You had the guts to stand up for justice, even in the face of family who disagreed with you. I want to be your friend, but it's up to you. Know this, though, whether you want to be friends or not doesn't matter because I will still consider you my friend."

Charlie waited for several seconds before pointing the barrel of his shotgun at the ground. "What are you looking for?"

Hank looked back at Abraham. "Tell him whose shirts you believe are on the line over there."

The colored boy stepped up alongside Hank. All the emotions from moments earlier were gone, replaced by a soft, non-accusing tone. "I followed you here because you were wearing my pappy's favorite shirt, but you went in the house before I could talk with you. That's when I noticed three more shirts hanging on the line facing the street. They look like the ones my pappy had with him when he came this way looking for work. I just want to look at them up close so I can see if they were his, if you'll let me."

"They're shirts. How will you know if they're his? I mean, my ma takes in wash for a living from a lot of different people. She's responsible for the laundry she takes in. What am I supposed to tell Reverend Wyatt? He's the one who moved us here and is letting us rent this house from him real cheap. We owe him a lot. Heck, he's still helping us by sending people to ma to do their laundry. If it wasn't for him, we'd be out on the streets with nowhere to go. If these shirts are your daddy's, how am I supposed to explain they're not here anymore without getting us in a lot of trouble from the person who brought them to her?"

"Just let him look at them. We'll all work together to decide what to do next if there's a reason to."

Charlie nodded. "Which ones do you want to see?"

Abraham smiled. "Thank you. They're right over here."

The four boys walked together to the last three shirts drying on the line near the fence at the back of the yard. Abraham checked a couple of buttons on each of the shirts in question. Hank watched as his friend's smile broadened across his face with each verification. The colored boy nodded and looked back at the three white boys. "They're his, all three of them."

Daniel grinned as he turned toward Charlie. "You've got to let him have them. His dad's dead, Charlie. They're all he has left of him."

"He's dead? But how...?"

"Hank found his skeleton near the river close to his farm this summer. Beth Ann and I helped him find out who it was. One of the clues was the shirt on it. He'd been shot in the back. When we showed Abraham the shirt, he recognized it and showed us the proof."

"There was proof?"

"Yeah, come here, I'll show you." Abraham showed them all the four-leaf clover stitched under the collar of each shirt and the tiny symbols sewn under several buttons.

Hank gingerly ran his fingers over the uniquely crafted emblems. "Abraham, these are beautiful. Your ma is an artist with a needle and thread. No wonder they're so special to you."

Charlie's eyes were wide open. "Does the shirt I was wearing have these same symbols?"

"Go get it, and let's check."

Charlie left them to go inside the house. Hank scanned the length of the street visible from where they stood in the yard while Daniel chattered on about the turn this trip had taken. Hank's heart skipped a beat when he saw Uncle Will almost directly across the street from their position in the yard. He leaned against a large oak tree and chewed on what looked like a piece of grass, his gaze fixed on Hank until the screen door slammed shut.

Hank noticed Charlie no longer had the shotgun with him. Instead, he held up the shirt in front of him like a banner as he approached them. "They're all here, the clover under the collar and the others are under the buttons. I don't know what to say."

Hank caught movement in his peripheral vision. When he looked back at the tree, he watched his uncle's face change from nonchalance to white-faced terror. He knew the expression all too well from seeing it on Daniel's face more times than he cared to count.

Chapter 12

What's spooking him? Hank turned away from the street and looked at the shirts hanging on the line, mesmerized by the billowing fabrics. His thoughts busily recounted events from the summer and now, half listening to the conversation between Abraham and Charlie. His mind reeled with the potential reasons for the sudden change in Uncle Will's demeanor. Then his memory flashed to the skeleton tied to the tree near the river, exactly as he'd found it in June. *Wait...oh...! Could it be...no...surely he's not involved in the...*

He slowly turned his head to look where Uncle Will had been standing. The nerves in his legs and knees trembled, threatening to knock him off his feet. *Where'd he go?* He immediately searched both ways along the boardwalks of Broadway. Sweat moistened his scalp and underarms. He swallowed bile as his gut wrenched with the possibility his conclusions forced him to acknowledge. Something touched his shoulder. He jerked his head around so fast he almost lost his balance. "Daniel!"

"What's more interesting across the street than...?" Daniel's eyebrows pointed toward his hairline. "What's wrong? You look a little green. Well, actually..."

"I saw him again. He was standing under that big oak tree over there." He used his head to indicate the general direction.

Daniel leaned over to look around Hank, and then he returned to his original stance. His brows came together in deep furrows. "Who?" Instantly, his brows pointed up, again. "Oh, you mean your uncle? Are you sure?"

Hank looked back across the street, pointing at the tree. "Yes, he was there, watching us; and he reacted when he saw Charlie with the shirt Abraham had seen him wearing." Hank turned his focus in the direction of Abraham and Charlie.

"How'd he react?"

"He was scared, really scared. I'm beginning to think he knows more about Mr. Blackman than he admitted to me. With Abraham confirming those shirts belonged to his pa, do you understand all the implications?"

"Yeah, Charlie's mom does laundry for the man who might have killed Mr. Blackman, and your uncle…." Daniel's eyes opened wide. "Wait…" He shook his head. "Surely you don't think your uncle's involved, do you?"

"Maybe, but I don't know for sure. At the very least, he could be the one who dropped those shirts off. I think it's safe to say he knows something. As far as I'm concerned, the critical question right now is this: why is he so afraid?"

"Well, maybe he knows the killer. I mean, think about it. Who else around here, besides us, is concerned about the death of a colored man?"

"I hope you're right, for Ma's sake."

"What did the deputy say when you told him you saw your uncle?"

"I haven't told him yet. He'd already left City Hall by the time I got there. I'll tell him when we meet up for lunch."

"What are you going to tell him about your face?"

Hank's mind flashed through the incident behind the theater in an instant. "What I keep telling *you*. I fell."

Daniel looked at him through squinted eyes for several seconds. "Umm-hmm, okay."

"What? You don't believe me?"

"No, I mean, yeah, I believe you, but I also think there's more you're not saying about it."

"Well, I think, right now, we need to get back to what's going on here with Charlie. We'll discuss Uncle Will more on the way home."

* * * * * * *

Hank put a hand on Charlie's shoulder. "Look, Charlie, no one's accusing you of anything, but we need some answers. You can help."

"I understand, but what can I do? We need the money, and I don't want to put my mom in danger. From what you're telling me, the man who brought these here could be a killer. I haven't seen the man who gave me the striped shirt since he gave it to me. How am I supposed to help you?"

"How does your ma know whose clothes are whose?"

"She keeps a ledger."

"Can you get it and see who brought these shirts to her?"

"Probably, but what do we do with the shirts? They belong to Abraham, but if the man who brought them notices them missing, what will happen to my mom?"

Daniel cleared his throat. "Hank, I think we need to find Deputy Collins and see what he can do."

"We could do that. What do you say, Charlie? Are you willing to talk with him and let him help?"

The boy put his hands on his hips and looked at the ground for several seconds. "Go ahead. Get him, but we have to keep my mom out of it."

"Good. Daniel, you and Abraham stay here. There's no need for all of us to go. I'll find Mr. Pete and bring him back as soon as possible."

* * * * * * *

It took Hank nearly half an hour to find the deputy. He nearly bumped right into the man as he came out of Goldman's Store with a package under his arm.

"Whoa, Hank; be careful, son. What's the hurry?"

The deputy's furrowed brows deepened when his focus shifted to Hank's facial scratches and the bump on his forehead.

"And what happened to your face?"

"Mr. Pete, I've been looking all over for you. I need you to come with me."

As they made their way back to Charlie's house, Hank explained the situation with Abraham's discovery and the dilemma surrounding the circumstances.

"You do realize I have no jurisdiction here, don't you?"

"Yes, sir, I do. We just need your advice for what to do with what we know."

* * * * * * *

Abraham showed the deputy the hidden emblems on the shirts hanging on the clothesline as well as the striped shirt he had draped over his shoulder— proof they had belonged to his father.

"Okay, first of all, you're right. This is serious. The evidence is solid, but until we know for sure who had possession of these shirts when they were brought here, we can't do much. And just because the person who brought them to be washed had them doesn't mean he had anything to do with Mr. Blackman's death, boys."

"What about my mom, deputy?"

"Well, that's the other thing. Is she home so we can see her records?"

"Yes, sir, but she doesn't know anything about what we've discovered here. I want to keep her from being any more involved than as it stands right now. She's been through enough without adding more to what's left of our family. I mean no disrespect, but…"

"I understand, son. I don't want to cause her any trouble either, but we need to get to the bottom of this for both of your safety."

"Yes, sir, she's inside. We can talk on the back porch."

"That's fine. It shouldn't take a lot of time to get the information I need."

* * * * * * *

Hank was impressed with Deputy Collins' tact with Mrs. Hutch and the situation surrounding Abraham's shirts. She was cooperative and forthright with all his future stepfather needed to investigate the matter further without implicating her or Charlie. Before they left, he shared an idea for pacifying the man who left the shirts with her. The plan included returning the shirts to Abraham without alerting the man to any wrongdoing or bringing suspicion on her or Charlie.

The deputy stood and reached out to shake Mrs. Hutch's hand. "Thank you, ma'am, for the information. I appreciate your help. It means more than you know. Okay, boys, we have a few more things to do before we head home. Charlie, it's good to see you taking good care of your mom. You're a good man. If something comes up concerning this situation or you think of anything else, let me know when I get back to town in a few days. I'll make sure to check in with you while I'm here."

"All right; thank you, sir." The two shook hands.

Hank stepped up beside the deputy. "Mr. Pete, would it be all right if Charlie joins us for lunch?"

"Sure, if it's all right with you, ma'am. I'm buying."

"Mom?" A smile spread slowly across his face.

"Sure, honey. Just don't be away all afternoon."

"We'll be at the American Café."

"All right, thank you, sir, for being my boy's friend. He doesn't have many, you know, especially since..."

"Mom!" Charlie's cheeks were instantly red.

Hank felt his own cheeks heat up as he grinned. "I'm glad we ran into him."

The deputy put his arms around both boys' shoulders. "Okay, let's beat the crowd to the café, what do you say?"

Daniel put his hat back on his head. "Come on, Abraham. Let's get some rock candy and peanut brittle for the ride home from the First Baptist Church ladies before they run out. We'll meet you at the café, Deputy Collins."

* * * * * * *

Charlie and Daniel kept them all entertained with stories throughout their lunch. Even Abraham added a few stories of his own to the conversations. Hank couldn't remember when he'd laughed so hard or so much.

The deputy wiped his mouth and placed his napkin on the table. "Whew, this was fun, but as much as I'd like to stay longer, boys, we really need to go. Charlie, I'm glad you came with us. If you're ever in the Frenchport area, stop in and say hello. You're welcome any time."

"I'll do that, sir. Thank you for lunch. I'd like to help you load up your wagons if you'll let me."

"You really don't have to, but I won't stop you. I'm sure these guys won't either." The deputy grinned as he ruffled Hank's and Daniel's hair. "Let's get on out of here."

When they left the café, a cool, light breeze stirred the air. Hank shivered before putting on his duster. "I thought it would be warmer by now."

Daniel watched as fourteen yoked oxen pulled a wagon loaded with a huge piece of oilfield machinery toward the railroad. "Would you look at that?"

Abraham's jaw dropped open as he looked on.

The deputy's footfalls on the boardwalk broke their awe-inspired silence. "Come on, boys. Daylight's wasting. I told the ladies we'd be back before dark."

When Hank felt the familiar tingle at the nape of his neck, he rubbed it, searching for the source of his unease, not sure how to determine who could be watching him.

I'm glad it's time to leave. I've had about as much of Smackover as I care to have for one day. This wasn't exactly the trip I thought it would be. I hope Beth Ann is having a better day at her dad's clinic.

With Charlie's help, it took just a little more than an hour to load up both wagons and secure them for the trip home. Hank drove the Baker wagon as he and Daniel led the way back to Farmville. They were both quiet till they reached the top of the hill known as Cooterneck.

Daniel stretched his arms across the backrest. "Okay, I'm dying here. Now that we're alone, care to tell me what's going on with you? You said you were going to tell the deputy at lunch about seeing your uncle. Why didn't you?"

"I didn't want to spoil the fun we were having with Charlie. I'll tell him when we get back. Besides…"

"You're stalling."

Hank clamped his mouth shut and gave his best friend a sidelong look, unnerved by his unwavering stare.

"Don't be giving me that look. You know you ignored me when I mentioned it earlier and changed the subject altogether. Now I'm getting the feeling, when you say you'll talk to him later, you're telling me what you think I want to hear to get me to shut up about it. You ought to know me better than that."

Hank shifted in his seat, his face and neck prickling from the barbs his nerves added to his guilt.

"I think there's something you're not telling me. You'd better be glad Beth Ann isn't here. She'd punch you."

"You're right."

"I knew it."

"She'd punch me."

"Come on, Hank, this isn't like you at all. And while you're at it, why don't you tell me what really happened to your face? Did you really just fall, or did you have help?"

Hank sighed. "I guess…well…it's hard to put into words." He pursed his lips as anger began to stew in his belly. His words came out sharper than he intended. "Sorry, I don't mean to be short with you. The truth is…I'm afraid, terrified actually, and I don't know how to deal with it, okay? Are you satisfied?"

Daniel leaned forward and put his forearms on his legs, quiet for several seconds. When he spoke, his voice had a serious tone Hank hadn't heard in a while. "You're a kid, Hank. There's nothing wrong with being afraid. You've been through a lot this summer. You finally know what happened to your dad. You practically became a crusader for justice on behalf of your family, Abraham, Granny Rose, the people living at Beech Hill, and even Charlie. According to Beth Ann, you showed an amazing amount of bravery with every experience."

"She said that?"

"Yeah, she did."

"So what's your point?"

"Personally, I'm glad Deputy Collins is in your life, now. You need to let him be the adult, and let yourself be the kid for a change. You've had to grow up faster than any of us because of your dad's absence. If you think about it, that wasn't fair to you. You really don't know how to be a kid. It's a new experience for you. I'm here to tell you that being afraid is normal for us. My dad tells me all the time fear builds character."

For more than a minute, the only sounds accompanying Hank's thoughts were the mules' snorts, their rhythmic, clip-clopping hooves, and the wagon wheels rolling along the dirt road.

Then, without the ability to stop it, Hank burst out laughing. It started from the deep well of his gut and rumbled to the surface unrestrained. The mules skittered momentarily from the outburst of the unexpected noise, but Hank didn't lose control of them. He wiped tears from his eyes, grateful for the release from all the tension of the past couple of days. He knew immediately when an undeniable peace washed over his heart and soul.

"What's so funny all of a sudden?" His closest friend's humor had returned, and Daniel's eyes glistened as his grin widened.

"You're the best, you know that? You always know what to say to snap me back to reality. Thanks. I've bottled up so much emotionally I wouldn't allow myself to laugh. Then you come along and say what I need to hear to break the bottle. That's why you're my best friend. Don't take this wrong, but your dad is right. Your fears are making you into quite a character, Daniel."

They both heehawed for several minutes, and then...BANG!

Chapter 13

The explosion came from behind them. Hank acted without hesitation and tightened his grip on the reins as his mule team spooked into a gallop. He stood as he wrapped the leather straps around his hands once and pulled as hard as he could against the impulse of the terrified animals. Then he used a pumping action with the reins, in order to gradually regain control without harming the mules' mouths.

"Hang on, now, mules! Whoa, Toby…easy, Daisy May…whoa… easy…easy!"

About a quarter of a mile down the road, Hank finally pulled the team to a stop on the side of the road. He looked back and watched Mr. Pete pull his team alongside them. All four mules fought their bits as they snorted, stamped their heavy hooves, and breathed heavily from their exertion.

"Whoa…are you boys all right?" The deputy jumped down from his rig and grabbed the bridles on Hank's team. "Let's give these animals a few minutes to calm down before we go on. Good job on keeping your team from stampeding. You did everything right, son. Here…you lost your hat." He picked up Hank's hat from the ground where it had fallen after the team finally stopped.

Hank sat back on the bench, his knees giving out on him. He breathed so hard his lungs hurt. He nodded as he looked over at Mr. Pete, taking his hat from the man's outstretched arm with a shaky hand. "Thanks. I didn't think...I just...did what I thought was right."

"I'm very proud of you, son. A lot of men panic in situations like that one. You held your own and kept your head."

Hank was surprised with Mr. Pete's serene reaction to the whole incident.

How does he do that? How does he stay so calm, like it's just another normal day like every other day? Doesn't anything shake him up?

"Were we shot at, deputy?" Daniel put one hand over his heart and used the other to fan his pale face with his own hat.

Hank bit his lip in amusement and watched Mr. Pete try to hide a smile as his eyes flashed a moment of spontaneous humor.

The deputy looked back toward Smackover. "No, that was a blowout. It sounded like it came from over around Phillip's Camp. Come on, we need to check the teams and wagons. Then we need to move out." While Abraham checked their team's legs and tack, the deputy made sure Hank's load was still secure.

"I've heard blowouts from a distance, but never this close before. I thought for sure we were about to die." Color slowly returned to Daniel's face.

"Nah, we're alive and well, my young friend." The deputy chuckled. "Just shake it off and check the team so we can go home. Hank, let's check your wagon, too, son. You took quite a ride back there."

After jumping down from their buckboard, Daniel went to the mules while Hank made sure the load hadn't shifted or loosened, and then he checked the axles.

"Are we good to go, boys?"

"Yes, sir." They all three spoke in unison.

"All right, then. Let's go home. Take the lead, Hank."

"Yes, sir."

* * * * * * *

Hank's mind reeled from the events of the day. *This is one day I definitely want to end...and sooner rather than later.* He thought about the warning Uncle Will gave him about there being eyes and ears everywhere and being careful who he talked to.

I need to talk to Daniel, but will it be safe for us to talk while we're on the road? How much do I tell him and the others? I don't want them in danger, but I know they can help, and I trust them. What do I do, Daddy?

"Hey...did you hear what I said?"

Hank jerked his head toward Daniel. "What? Uh...no...sorry, I...."

"See, this is what I was talking about. Whatever is going on inside that head of yours is too important to wait for everyone to be together. You need to talk to me."

"I know, but...I will..." Hank thought he saw movement in the trees to his left. He scanned the woods on either side of the road before lowering his voice to a whisper. "I just need to make sure it's safe."

"Safe...?"

"Shhh...keep your voice down."

"What do you mean by 'safe,' and why are we whispering?"

"Because I was told I was being watched and that they knew things..."

"Huh? Who told you? Who is 'they,' and when did 'they'... wait...what do they know?"

"That's what I'm trying to tell you, but..." Hank checked the woods again. "Look, I have a lot to tell you and something to show you, but we have to be careful. For now, you need to wait. Be patient. When we get to the crossroads and turn toward

Frenchport, we should be safe. I'll tell you what's going on then, okay? We're too close to Smackover for my comfort."

"All right, but no more stalling."

"I promise."

They rode in silence for a couple of minutes.

"You do realize how long you're making me wait, don't you?"

"Sorry, but you'll understand when it's all out in the open."

"Now you've *really* got my curiosity stirred up. I don't know if I can wait till the crossroads. There are at least a thousand questions already coming to mind."

"Yeah, well, I'm telling you, this was not the trip I had expected it to be."

"You're telling me? What about Abraham? Who knew we'd run into Charlie Hutch? For that matter, what do you think of his explanation for why those shirts were on his mama's clothesline?"

"I'm thinking there's more than we've put together so far."

"You don't mean your uncle, do you?"

"I don't know, but maybe. You didn't see his face when Charlie brought out that striped shirt. He looked like he'd seen a ghost or something. Just let me think for a few more miles, so I can put things in perspective. Then we'll talk, and you can help me figure out how to tell Beth Ann and Abraham."

"And just what do you propose I do while you're thinking?"

"Well, do what you do best. What would Sherlock Holmes do?"

"But you haven't given me anything specific to work with."

"I can't...yet."

Daniel let out a puff of breath before he folded his arms over his chest. Then he lowered his hat over his eyes. "Fine, since I don't have a violin, I'll take a nap. Wake me up when you're ready to talk."

* * * * * * *

The more Hank thought about all that had happened in Smackover, the more he wondered about possible connections: the dream, the escaped prisoners, running into Uncle Will, the key, and finding shirts that belonged to Mr. Blackman. Then he thought about Mr. Morgan. *Is he mixed up in all of this? Why else was he so antsy? Why leave so abruptly? Nothing makes sense.* Before he knew it, he found himself thinking of his daddy.

I wish you were here. How is it I could hear you speak to me before we finally learned you were dead? No matter what I asked you, your answer or advice was always right. Did I do something wrong to make you go completely silent?

The voice came so suddenly, Hank was startled by it. *Trust your heart and not your eyes, son. Act wisely because there will be times you'll need to trust your eyes and not your heart.*

"That's you, Daddy?"

Daniel sucked in a long breath. "Huh, did you say something?" He stretched and yawned.

"Uh…no, just thinking out loud, I guess. Sorry I woke you."

"Where are we?"

"Just about at the crossroads, so I guess it's a good thing you're awake."

"That didn't take long."

"Have you ever wondered why it seems to take less time to get home than it does to go somewhere?"

"What do you mean?"

"Well, think about it. Didn't it seem to take forever to get to Smackover this morning? But the drive home seems to be quicker. The distance is the same, and we have loaded wagons this time. But it doesn't matter because the trip is faster for some reason."

"You're right. Huh! That is odd."

"Are you awake enough to talk?"

"Sure."

"We're far enough from Smackover, but just to be safe, we need to keep our voices down. Where do you want me to start?"

"Tell me about seeing your uncle, why you didn't tell the deputy, what happened to your face, and..."

Hank nodded vigorously. "Okay, okay..."

"Don't even think about leaving anything out."

Daniel listened without interruption except for a few questions every now and then for clarification. Hank knew his friend was processing the information, initiating his inductive reasoning skills to better understand the events. He emulated his hero, Sherlock Holmes, in this kind of instance perfectly. Hank admired that in him and trusted his instincts, doubting neither his ability nor his conclusions.

"Do you think any of this has to do with your dream?"

"I'm not sure. It's like my mind keeps niggling at me to find the connection where there isn't an obvious one."

"Maybe Beth Ann will see it. She's pretty sharp about catching the little things we overlook sometimes."

Hank smiled. "Why Daniel, did you just..."

His lifelong friend grinned. "Yeah, yeah, but don't you dare tell her I did."

"If I didn't know better, I'd say you're beginning to see her in a different light."

"Don't go there. She's more like a sister than anything else. Besides, if you knew the truth, you'd..."

"What truth?"

Daniel pursed his lips.

"Why'd you stop? Finish your sentence."

He hid his face behind his hat, but not before Hank saw how red it was. "Nope, I can't. I promised."

Hank grinned.

"If she knew I had said even that little bit, she'd…"

He waited several seconds. "She'd what?"

"I'm changing the subject now." He replaced his hat on his head. "Do you think Charlie told us everything he knows about those shirts?"

Hank gave his friend a sidelong glance. "If he didn't, I'm sure Mr. Pete will be able to get it out of him. For now, I'm just glad he isn't hostile toward us. He's not like his brother or dad, but he's protective of his family, what's left of it anyway. If anyone understands that role, I do."

"True."

"I'm glad he did the right thing and gave the shirts to Abraham."

"Me, too."

Neither said anything else for several minutes as they rounded the final curve before getting to the turn-off to the Baker farm. Hank felt the mules pick up their pace. Just like when they come in from plowing or working the fields, the animals sensed home and sped up on their own.

"So I was thinking we should probably meet in our hay loft until things settle down. If Uncle Will isn't bluffing and there are people watching me and listening in on our conversations, we should probably stay away from our fishing hole. Besides, with it getting colder now, it'll be warmer in the barn."

"Yeah, I've been thinking about all those times you felt someone was watching us. You were probably right, especially after what your uncle said. Are you going to talk with Deputy Collins about any of this?"

"I need to tell him about Uncle Will."

"What about the key?"

"Let's keep that to ourselves for right now."

"You mean just you and me?"

"Yeah, it may turn out to be nothing."

"What do you think the deputy will do with the information about the shirts?"

"I don't know for sure, but I believe he'll do the right thing by Abraham and his family."

As they pulled into the drive of the Baker farm, Mr. Pete and Abraham pulled up alongside them.

"Okay, boys, it looks like we have about an hour and a half of daylight left. Do you want help unloading, Hank?"

"What do you think, Daniel? Can we get it ourselves?"

"Sure."

"We'll get it. You two go on to Granny's."

"Very good, then, you're on your own. Be sure to feed and rub down the mules after you unhitch them."

"Yes, sir."

"I'll be back to take you home before chores and supper, Daniel."

"Sure thing, deputy."

They watched Granny's wagon turn onto the road before Hank drove to the green house— a large, two-room shack covered with green, rolled roofing material. The Bakers used it for storing small farm equipment, supplies, staples, Ma's canned goods, feed for the livestock, and gardening tools. The boys worked without saying much, other than where to put and stack the supplies and goods they had picked up in Smackover. When they finished putting away the wagon and taking care of the mules, the sun was still about thirty minutes from going down.

"Want to come in and wait for Mr. Pete?"

"Sure, but I need a drink first."

"I'll be in my room." Hank went into the house from the back porch, not waiting for Daniel to pump water from the well in the yard. As he entered the kitchen, his scalp tingled. He stopped just inside the door and looked around, rubbing the nape of his neck, his brows furrowed. "Ma...Jimmy...?"

Silence. *Of course, there's no answer. They're still at Granny's.*

He ignored his itchy scalp as he remembered having the same feeling this morning when he couldn't find his new hat. He *knew* he had put it on the nail just inside the closet. *So where is it?* He forced himself to take calm, deliberate steps down the hallway to his room. When he opened the door, he immediately noticed it on his bed. All the blood drained from his face as dizziness threatened to knock him off his feet and darkness edged its way into his peripheral vision.

Chapter 14

Hank steadied himself as he held tightly onto the doorknob. He swallowed hard, past the lump in his throat, and blinked until his vision cleared. *My new hat! It was in the closet last night, but not this morning. Where...?* He felt the hair on his neck and around his ears bristle as his skin tingled. He began to hyperventilate. *Some...I wasn't crazy this morning...someone* was *in the house...*

Then he noticed something sticking out from under the brim. He took tentative steps to the bed and saw it was a folded piece of paper before he retrieved it. *Another note?* His hands shook as he opened it and recognized the penmanship. Like the first note, there was no signature. The letters were similar in shape and size to the one he'd found on the porch post. And like the other note, there was something disturbing and ominous about the message:

WE KNOW HOW TO GET TO YOU, HANK. YOU HAVE SOMETHING THAT BELONGS TO US. WE KNOW YOU TOOK IT, AND WE WANT IT BACK. LEAVE IT ON THE ROCK AT YOUR FISHING HOLE BY SUNDOWN TOMORROW.

He spun around and bolted from his room. He and Daniel collided in the hallway and reacted in unison. "Aaaaahhhh!"

"Hey, didn't you hear me come in?"

"Daniel! Get out of here!"

Hank led the retreat through the kitchen and screened-in back porch, down the steps into the yard, and finally to the sweet gum tree in the driveway. He leaned against the rough bark and wiped his brow with his forearm, realizing he still had the note in his hand.

Daniel tripped over an exposed tree root and fell a few feet from where Hank rested. He picked himself up and slapped dirt from his shirt and trousers legs. "I don't think I've ever seen you this scared. What happened? What's that in your hand?" His voice cracked as his words slurred a bit, his breathing heavy and shaky.

Hank stared at the note. "I found it in my room." Then he looked up, terror paralyzing his ability to think rationally for more than a few seconds at a time. "It's not good. Someone's been here while we were away."

"What?"

"It's the only thing that makes sense. When I went in for my hat this morning, I couldn't find my new one where I had put it. I had the feeling...well...." He unfolded the note and silently read it again. "When I went to my room just now, it was on my bed with this note under it. The writing's the same as the other one. Do you know what this means?" Tears stung Hank's eyes, but he refused to allow them to fall. "Daniel, someone's been here, inside the house, while we were in Smackover. It's highly probable he was here while we were at Granny's, too. What if we hadn't gone...?"

Daniel grabbed Hank's shoulders. "Hey, stop it! You need to calm down before you give yourself a heart attack!"

Hank nodded and took a couple of deep breaths. "See what I mean? I'm panicking here. This is crazy. I never panic. What's wrong with me?"

"It's okay. You're not crazy. You'll be fine. You're a kid, remember? But you still have to get control of yourself. Now, without over-reacting, I need to ask you a question."

"I'll try."

"Good. Do you think he's still...you know...?"

Hank looked past his friend at the house. "I don't know. That's why we're out here, just in case."

"Okay, you're doing just fine." Daniel took a couple of steps back, his arms akimbo. "Now, let me read the note."

Hank timidly handed it to him and watched his face. When his friend finished reading it, he refolded it and gave it back, his brows furrowed and his cheeks red. He crossed his arms over his chest.

"Do you think they're talking about the key?"

Hank put the note in his coat pocket. "How could they? I didn't have it until I broke the chain off Uncle Will's neck this morning, while we were in Smackover. I really don't..." Hank's mind flashed to the whiskey he'd buried in the woods. "Wait a minute...no..." He scratched the top of his head.

"What are you thinking?"

"I'm not absolutely positive, but...what if...well...I guess it's possible they're talking about some whiskey I dug up before I was kidnapped in June. It's actually *why* I was kidnapped in the first place. There were G-men looking for some they claimed Uncle Will had hidden on our farm. When I found it, I reburied it in the woods so Ma wouldn't get in trouble. Other than that, I really can't think of what they want me to give back."

"Maybe the deputy can help."

As if on cue, they turned toward the sound of a motor car coming around the bend from Granny's place. They watched it turn onto the Baker property.

"For now, don't say anything. I'll talk with Mr. Pete about Uncle Will after we take you home. I need a little more time to think about how and when to tell him about the notes, but I will, I promise."

"What about the deadline?"

"Without knowing what they want exactly, what can I do?"

"Maybe you should tell the deputy about this note at least. Then he can set a trap and catch whoever is behind it. What if it's the escaped prisoner?"

"Good point. Just let me handle it, okay?"

"For now, but don't wait much longer. This is way more serious than we could have imagined."

* * * * * * *

Hank was glad Mr. Pete was preoccupied with driving instead of looking at him while he told him about his encounter with Uncle Will.

"Why didn't you tell me this while we were in Smackover?"

Hank looked at his clasped hands in his lap, his thumbs pushing hard against one another, but he hardly noticed the pain. "I went looking for you at City Hall to tell you, but you'd already left. When I saw you next, I'd forgotten about it. Besides, I'd only seen him a couple of times from a distance. He *looked* like Uncle Will, but he *didn't* look like him."

"What's *that* supposed to mean?"

In his peripheral vision, Hank saw Mr. Pete look over at him briefly then back at the road ahead. "Well, there was something about him that didn't seem to fit right. I don't know. I can't say exactly what was different, but there was something."

"Okay, and you only saw him from a distance?"

"Yes, sir, and when he crossed the street, he was fast. So I really can't be sure if it was him or not."

Mr. Pete sighed heavily. "All right, but you have to promise you'll keep looking for me in the future if you see him again. Keep looking till you find me, so I can get to the bottom of this."

"Yes, sir, I will." Hank felt the deputy look at him, a little longer this time, before he returned his attention to the road.

"What about your face? You never really explained what happened when I asked you in town."

Hank looked out the side window. "Someone shoved me, and I fell when I was headed to City Hall." *It's what happened...kind of.*

"You didn't see who it was?"

He looked at Mr. Pete's profile, hoping the fading light of dusk kept the deputy from seeing his blushing face if he decided to look back at him. "No, sir, you saw the crowds."

When they arrived back at the Baker farm to take care of the evening chores, Mr. Pete parked under the old tree beside the driveway and turned off the engine. For a couple of minutes, neither of them spoke or moved. They simply sat and gazed out the windshield until the deputy broke the silence.

"I wish you had found me, son. Your safety is more important to me than any errand I needed to run. There are some really bad men out there looking for you. Please don't take that lightly."

Hank noticed nothing out of the ordinary as he scanned his family's property. "I won't." *Well, that went better than I thought, but shouldn't I feel better?* Suddenly, Daniel's words resounded in his head. *Maybe you should tell the deputy about this note at least.*

"Good, now let's get the chores done. Granny said supper would be ready in about an hour when I left. If we're late, she'll make us watch everyone else eat sweet potato pie."

Hank was relieved to see Mr. Pete smiling. He smiled too, but his stomach felt somewhat unsettled.

"Yes, sir, I'll start in the henhouse."

* * * * * * *

No matter how tired Hank felt when the family returned home, sleep evaded him. Every time the house creaked his eyes popped open, his body stiff with fear. He almost wet his pants when Jimmy's snoring sounded like someone opening their bedroom door. His mind raced from seeing Uncle Will to the encounter with him behind the theater and then finding the hat on his bed.

The last mental reenactment automatically made him think about the notes, especially the latest one.

What do I have that they want? They can't possibly know about the key, can they? And what's so special about the whiskey? It's not like they can't get more.

A noise outside caught his attention. He sat up slowly and crept to his window, making sure he didn't stir the curtain as he peeked between it and the edge of the sill. He spied a couple of armadillos chasing one another across the yard toward the tree in the driveway. He didn't realize he'd held his breath till he let it out.

As he lay back down on his pillow, he thought about the note left on the post near the porch steps. *"Like father, like son."* All of a sudden, Hank sat up. His heart skipped a couple of beats. His uncle's words came back to him with thunderous intensity.

I really wish you hadn't seen me. This complicates things more than you can imagine, for you as well as for me. You really are your father's son, aren't you? He had a way of making things difficult, too.

"The first note was from him…Uncle Will. But what did he mean when he said Daddy 'made things difficult, too'?" Subconsciously, he knew his ears needed to hear the whispered words in order to process their meaning. He just didn't want to disturb his brother.

Hank heard Jimmy stir. He carefully leaned back against his headboard so as not to wake him, and then he listened, wide-eyed, as his brother spoke gibberish before settling, again. Once all was still, Hank lay down and closed his eyes, not expecting to sleep with his mind so rampant with wild ideas mixed with real events from the past couple of days. When he opened his eyes, it was daybreak.

* * * * * * *

While the preacher droned on with his sermon, Hank switched back and forth between staring at the backs of each of his friends' heads. Neither Daniel nor Beth Ann moved, except Daniel when he scratched the top of his head. Hank tried to will them to look at him, but it was no use.

What am I doing? If that had worked, I can hear Daniel now. He'd be sure, beyond a shadow of a doubt, that I was possessed by Granny Rose's evil spirit. Just wait till after church. It's not like you can talk to them now, anyway.

Suddenly, everyone jumped in unison as Pastor Bob pounded his fist on the pulpit. Hank's heart nearly stopped beating altogether. It was like God had clapped his hands in front of his face to gain his undivided attention. From that point on, he stayed focused on the message from the pastor.

"Hear me, friends. God is in charge of all that happens because he is God and we are not. It really doesn't matter whether you believe it or not. Will people disappoint you? Yes, they will. Is life fair? No, it is not. Will we find the answers to all of our questions? No, we will not. That's life as we know it.

"Dear ones, the fact of the matter is this. We live in a fallen world among fallen people, but there is hope and a purpose for each and every one of us. For those who put their faith and trust in the Creator and his redemptive work, there is hope and peace. Everything else fails to meet this need in our hearts and lives. He wants a relationship with you. Won't you accept his invitation? Now is the accepted time. Let's pray."

The rest of the service was a blur as Hank contemplated how to proceed with his own situation with the help of his friends. He had chosen not to tell Mr. Pete everything, but he did tell the deputy what he thought law enforcement needed to know for now. However, Beth Ann and Abraham needed to know everything. Then the four of them could divide up the remaining tasks to help with the investigation without being in Mr. Pete's way. Time was of the essence. They needed to meet that afternoon. School would be a factor over the next several days, but they'd deal with it. After all, it was no longer summer vacation.

As soon as church let out, Beth Ann and Daniel found Hank by the gate to the cemetery. They agreed to meet in the Baker hayloft around three o'clock that afternoon, giving Hank plenty of time to make sure Abraham was with them. Then Hank heard Mr. Pete call to him from the truck. "I've got to go. See you this afternoon." He ran to where his family waited.

"Ma, Beth Ann and Daniel are coming over later this afternoon."

"Today's not a good day, son. Pastor Bob is coming by to talk with all of us about the wedding and what you and I talked about yesterday."

"Okay. Just let me tell them real quick. I'll be right back." He ran back to his friends.

Beth Ann's smile faded. "Is something wrong?"

"Yeah, we have to wait till tomorrow to talk. We have company coming this afternoon, and I have to be there."

Daniel crossed his arms over his chest. "I don't want to meet at school. We really need to include Abraham."

"Good point." Beth Ann shielded her eyes from the sun as she looked in Hank's direction. "Why don't we meet in your hayloft after school? Besides, we'll have more time then than we would at lunch."

Hank nodded. "I'll run over to Granny's right after we eat and tell him the plan. If there's a problem, I'll let you know tomorrow."

"Okay, see you at school."

As Beth Ann left the group, Daniel grabbed Hank's arm. "What about the deadline? It's at sundown today, isn't it?"

"Yeah, but I still don't know what I'm supposed to give back. I've got to go. I'll see you tomorrow."

"Be careful, Hank. I don't think those guys are fooling around. You did tell the deputy about the note, didn't you?"

"I've got to go, Daniel. We'll talk tomorrow."

"Hank…"

"Tomorrow…"

Chapter 15

When Hank walked out of the woods between the Baker property and Granny's farm, Pastor Bob's empty buggy was parked in the driveway, the horse tied to the hitching post. *Doggone it, I'm late. Ma's going to have my hide.* He ran the rest of the distance to the back porch. As he entered through the kitchen door, he heard laughter from the front parlor. Hank tossed his hat on his bed as he quickly tiptoed past his room. Then he stopped a moment to take a couple of deep breaths, and to run his fingers through his hair before joining the family meeting with their company.

"Sorry, I'm late, Ma. I got back as fast as I could." Hank sat on his hands as he took a seat on the cool hearth.

"It's okay, son; Pastor Bob and Miss Tootsie just got here, too."

Hank nodded and returned the couple's smiles.

Ma sat with her spine straight and slightly away from the back of the divan as she held Mr. Pete's hand. "Thank you so much for coming by today. We appreciate your taking the time to talk with us and discuss the wedding."

"I'm happy to, Martha. There are a lot of people around here wondering what took you two so long to realize what they already knew. It seems yours is a match made in heaven, so to speak."

Hank watched as if he were on the outside looking in as everyone else in the room chuckled.

Mr. Pete patted Ma's hand with his free hand and winked at her before turning his attention back to the pastor. His grin spread across his face, his brows pointing toward his hairline. "Actually, we were afraid people would think it was too quick. After all, it's only been a few months since we first met."

"Well, when it's right, time doesn't always count, I guess. How long has it been, Martha, since Charles left for the war?"

She sat back before answering. "My goodness, he's been gone right about eight years in all. A little more than seven years ago, he was declared 'missing in action,' but he left home almost a year before that."

Hank felt his heart pinch from the impact of her words. *But he's really been gone only a few months, Ma. It's been since we...*

"What about you, Pete? I understand you've had your own waiting period."

He nodded. "Yes, sir, my wife died in childbirth eight and a half years ago."

What? For the second time in just a few moments, Hank found himself distracted by a disturbing declaration. *He's a widower? Why didn't he...?*

"Jimmy Jack, I think I know your opinion concerning your ma and Pete getting married. But I'd like to hear it from you for myself."

Jimmy sat hunched over in the middle of the floor with his legs crisscrossed, his hands clasped. His eyes sparkled as his grin widened. "Well, it seems like I've been waiting for him my whole life. I mean, I know he's not my real daddy, but I already think of him like he is." He shrugged his shoulders. "I can't help it. It's like we had this big, huge, gigantic hole in our family before he came along. Then we didn't."

Hank listened to more chuckles as he stared at his brother. His face reddened as he looked around and realized he was the only one somber.

"How about you, Hank; what are your concerns? You seem to be a little troubled by this discussion."

He looked from Ma to Mr. Pete and back to his ma before answering, his heart aching. Then he focused on the pastor. "Um, no…but, uh…well, I have to be honest. It's different for me than it is for Jimmy because I *do* remember Daddy and what it was like having him around. And…well…I really, really miss him sometimes." He fought to keep tears from rolling down his face and tried to keep his voice strong and steady. "In the beginning, it was hard for me when Mr. Pete came calling so much, and it took a while to get used to him being here instead of Daddy, you know? But…"

Hank felt everyone's stares on him as his pause stretched into several seconds. He was grateful no one rushed him. He scratched his cheek then his scalp as he looked at Mr. Pete. The man's expression was both warm and kind as he smiled and nodded at Hank. "Well, I had to realize this isn't just about me. I had to think of the whole family. Like Jimmy said, we were incomplete. Ma's great, but she's not a dad. The older I get, the more I understand she needs something my brother and I can't give her. And we need someone she can't be.

"I know she gets lonely, especially when she's around other couples and she has to come home alone. You know…without another adult…a husband…in the house. I guess I was kind of worried her relationship with Mr. Pete would become more important to her than us. But she's never let that happen, and neither does he.

"Now she's different. She laughs and sings around the house. The changes in her haven't changed our family…well…except to make us closer to one another, I think. I'm really glad Ma is happy. I know it's because of Mr. Pete. He loves her…and us… Jimmy and me, that is.

"I still struggle with believing Daddy's gone forever, but Mr. Pete is patient. He helps me when I'm sad, when really strong emotions try to control me, and when I'm experiencing feelings I don't understand."

Hank sat up tall as he made direct eye-contact with Mr. Pete. "I'd like to tell you something if I may. Actually, I *need* to tell you something, and I don't mind who hears it or who knows it anymore." He blew out a long breath. "You're…you're like Daddy in a lot of ways. I was uncomfortable with that at first because I didn't like admitting it, but now, I like it…a lot." He pursed his lips to keep them from quivering and swallowed a sob before continuing. "I guess you could say you're growing on me, and I'm learning to love you like a father. Eventually, I'd like to call you 'dad,' but I can't… not yet. I only had one daddy. I need to get used to him not coming back…ever. I hope you understand. I just need you to give me a little more time." He wiped a single tear from his cheek.

The deputy took a handkerchief from his pants pocket and wiped his own eyes. "You take as long as you need, son. I do understand." His voice had a slight tremor in it. "My love for you doesn't depend on how you feel about me. We'll work together to be the family you want."

Hank nodded and clenched his teeth for a few seconds, trying to keep a wave of tender emotions from drowning him in the moment. "That's all, pastor."

The sound of soft sniffles came from all around the room.

Pastor Bob leaned forward in his chair and clasped his hands as he rested his elbows on his legs. "From what I'm hearing and what I'm seeing, you all have already begun the process of becoming a united family. That's wonderful. It's the toughest part of a second marriage where there are children. I see no reason to postpone anything, so I'll add the wedding to my calendar for the first of

November. As for the ceremony itself, I'll meet with just the two of you for those details later. Before we're done here today, it's my understanding there is another issue that's come up. And you want to discuss it while everyone is present. Is that right, Martha?"

Ma nodded, looking quickly at Mr. Pete before she looked back at the pastor. "Yes, I…well…I have questions…about the grieving process. I mean, I spent several years grieving over Charles' absence while he was missing. In fact, I felt in my heart he was most likely dead, and considered myself a widow long before it was confirmed. But when my suspicions proved true, it felt like salt had been poured onto a wound in my soul that hadn't healed."

She fiddled with her handkerchief in her lap as she stared at it. "It was like I had never grieved at all." She looked toward the pastor and his wife. "Is this normal? Will it ever finally end? I truly believed I had dealt with everything to completion. I was ready to…I want so much to…move on with my life. Then, just the other day, I found myself distraught because I realized…"

When Ma still hadn't completed her sentence after several seconds and fresh tears flowed down her cheeks, Mr. Pete covered her clasped hands with one of his. His voice sounded sad as he looked into her eyes. "You…still love him, don't you?"

Ma dabbed at her eyes with her handkerchief and then nodded, but she didn't look at him. "Yes. I'm…I'm sorry, but…"

"You feel you've betrayed him because you love me, too?"

She blew her nose and nodded.

Deputy Collins looked at the pastor. "If you don't mind, Bob, I'd like to answer her questions."

He nodded. "Sure, go ahead."

Mr. Pete looked at Ma and spoke, to Hank's surprise, as if no one else were in the room. "Honey, look at me." He waited for her to comply. He caressed the side of her face with his free hand, and used his fingers to push her hair behind her ear before holding her hands in both of his. "I can tell you with complete assurance…

your feelings are very normal. There's no right or wrong way to mourn. There are no two people who will ever experience it *exactly* the same way. The truth is it hurts like no other pain in the world. And even though you are not alone in this pain, no one will *ever* be able to know what you are going through because we're all different. There are only two things we can know and honestly understand about the grieving process. First, it's more painful than any physical injury, and second, it's a path we can't avoid.

"As for grieving the loss of your soul mate, I can tell you I understand what you are dealing with because I'm on that same journey myself. I've discovered there is no set time to mourn, and then it's over. I'm convinced it will probably *never* end. Some days it feels like it'll take forever. Then there are other days it feels like it's finally done when something unexpected hits out of the blue, like an emotional bomb waiting to explode. Just about anything can trigger it—a smell, a sound, or a mistaken identity. The first time I saw someone I thought was Rachel, I thought I would die. It hurt so much, worse than the first time almost, to have her that close and lose her all over again. But it wasn't her."

He paused to wipe his eyes and blow his nose. "I still struggle with my own grief over her loss and that of our tiny, baby boy." Mr. Pete dried his wet face. Then he took Ma's hands again, and kissed them. "It's the hardest thing I've ever had to face, and there is a lot of fear attached to it sometimes because it's something I have to do alone. But you already know that. For whatever reason, even though we don't understand why, we're still alive while they had to leave us.

"The love I have for Rachel and your love for Charles…it doesn't just dissolve with them because they're dead. I believe love is forever. There is one thing we have to be careful to guard against, though—guilt. It started haunting me from the moment I knew I was falling in love with you. I almost ran away from it until I realized what I would be giving up. So I've had to learn to ignore any 'guilty' feelings because they're not healthy. Our commitments to be faithful to Rachel and Charles are completed. That part has changed, but not our love for them. Please believe me. I don't feel threatened by your love for Charles because I know *exactly* how you feel.

"Once I realized you made me feel whole again, I knew you were the one who could help me heal from the worst experience of my life. You and your boys have given me the gift of new life. You've helped me set aside the sadness over my loss so I am free to love again. You're not a duplicate of her or a replacement for what I've lost. You are a totally new fulfillment within for me. It's something no one else, not even Rachel, could give me. That's what I want...I want what you, and only you, can give me. When I found you, I learned how to fall in love again, and I know it's what she would want for me, too." He wiped his face again and sniffed.

"I know, in my heart, we are meant to be together. That's why I asked you to marry me. Will we continue to grieve after we're married? I don't know, but we'll have each other to deal with the feelings if, and when, they show up. I just know I love you, and I want to spend the rest of my life with you. And never doubt that I am more than happy to raise Charles' boys so they never forget him, whether they call me 'dad' or not." The deputy kissed Ma on the cheek and smiled. Then he nodded toward the pastor.

Once again, the sound of soft sniffles filled the room, and Hank felt a newfound respect for Mr. Pete well up inside his heart.

The pastor cleared his throat. "Martha, I couldn't have said it better myself. I have not experienced what you two have, concerning the deaths of your spouses, but I know true love when I see it. You have nothing to worry about."

Ma looked from the pastor to Mr. Pete and smiled through her tears. "I agree."

The grin on the deputy's face brightened the mood in the room. Hank found himself pondering what he had just witnessed and the words expressed by the one who would become his stepfather. He breathed deeply, puffing out his chest with sad pride for the developing relationship with this man so like his flesh and blood father. *I guess this is it, Daddy. He's here to stay, and I can't think of any reason to stop it.*

* * * * * * *

About half an hour later, everyone watched from the porch as Pastor Bob's buggy went around the bend at the end of the Baker driveway. Almost immediately, Sheriff Stan drove up and parked under the sweet gum tree. Hank's ears burned, and his pulse beat fast. *Oh, no!* When the sheriff got out of his motor car, his brows were furrowed and his mouth was set in a tight line.

"Looks like Stan has news. Stay here, boys, while your mom and I talk with the sheriff." Mr. Pete and Ma held hands as they met Sheriff Stan at the edge of the yard, their voices muffled.

When Ma glanced directly at Hank, he noticed she had the same expression of unrest on her face as the sheriff's when he arrived. He felt a chill spread from the inside out, and he felt his knees weaken. *Something's happened.* "I think I need to sit down, Jimmy." He went to the bench swing hanging from a rafter on the far side of the porch.

"Maybe it's good news."

"Not likely. Didn't you see their faces?"

"Not really. What do you suppose it's about?"

"My guess is it has something to do with Mr. Higgins, the escaped prisoner, or Uncle Will."

"I don't wish anything bad on you, but I hope it's not Uncle Will."

"I know."

Just then, the group meeting broke up, and Sheriff Stan left as Ma and Mr. Pete walked back to the porch.

Hank stood, the backs of his knees touching the wooden planks of the swing seat. He was afraid he'd fall if he stepped away from it. "What did the sheriff want?"

Mr. Pete breathed in deeply then let out a huff, his brows furrowed. "The news is troubling, to put it mildly, but I don't want you to worry. There's been a sighting of Al Higgins. He was seen in Camden late this afternoon, actually near Fairview School in the Cullendale area. He's alone. They're working under the assumption he's armed and very dangerous. It looked like he was heading this way. Police Chief Ellis has a posse looking for him now. He asked Stan and me to join them and be on the lookout for him. With it being late and getting dark, the biggest concern is his giving us all the slip before we know where he is exactly and not being prepared for what he's up to."

The deputy kissed Ma's hands. "If it's all right with you, sweetheart, I think I'll stay in the hayloft tonight and keep watch from there."

"Of course. Will you be warm enough out there?"

"Yeah, I just need to get my gear and weapon from Granny's. I don't think there's anything to worry about, but I don't want to take any chances. I also think it might be a good idea to keep the boys home from school, at least tomorrow."

Hank immediately thought about Beth Ann and Daniel. "But…"

"No arguments, son. Your safety is my biggest concern right now. I can't protect you there like I can here."

Hank nodded, a heavy weight on his shoulders. "Yes, sir."

"Good." He kissed Ma on the mouth. "Wait for me inside. I'll let you know when I get back."

"Please be careful."

"I will. Now, get inside so I know you're all safe while I'm gone."

* * * * * * *

Sleep was impossible. Hank lay on his back with his eyes wide open, listening to the grandfather clock chime every half hour till well after midnight. When he finally went to sleep, it wasn't deep. He woke often. Every time he awoke, he sat up to check on Jimmy's bed. Right after the clock struck two, Hank's eyes closed till just before dawn. When he looked over at his brother's bed, his nerves jolted him wide awake. *Where is he?* Immediately, the images from his dream flashed through his mind. He scrambled out of bed and rushed to the window. *Don't panic. Remember, Mr. Pete's in the hayloft.* His eyes took several seconds to adjust to the light just before sunrise.

He caught movement in his peripheral vision, near the outhouse. *Jimmy! You little dickens! I ought to...* Hank left the window and hurriedly got back in bed. He couldn't tell if his shivering was the result of the adrenaline flowing through his veins or the crisp morning air. He pulled the covers over him and curled up in a ball, trying to get warm while watching the bedroom door till Jimmy returned.

Finally, the door opened and he watched his little brother tiptoe back to his bed. Through chattering teeth Hank scolded him. "What do you think you were doing going to the outhouse?"

"Uh, what do you think?"

Jimmy lay back on his pillow and pulled the covers up to his neck.

"Are you crazy? That's why we have a chamber pot in our room. That escaped prisoner is in the area. Didn't you hear Mr. Pete last night? You could have been..."

"Didn't you hear him yourself? He's in the barn, keeping watch."

"Jimmy..."

"Hank.... Why are you talking funny?"

Hank turned his back on his brother, tears forming in his eyes. "Never mind, you wouldn't understand." *Get control of yourself, Hank. Maybe he's better off naïve.*

It was quiet for several seconds. When Jimmy's voice came from near Hank's covered head, his raw nerves made his vision flash white as he bounced what seemed like several inches off his bed.

"I'm sorry." Jimmy touched his big brother on the shoulder.

"I didn't think you'd be this worried. You're really jumpy."

Hank yanked away from the touch. "I'm fine."

"Then why are you so angry?"

Calm down. He's not to blame for this. "I'm not angry, just sc..."

"What?"

Hank uncovered his head and turned so he could see his brother. "I'm all right. It's just that I was...concerned when I didn't see you in bed, okay?"

"Okay."

Hank turned on his back and closed his eyes. "I'm sorry, little brother. I didn't mean to yell at you. You didn't do anything wrong." He sat up and patted his bed. "Sit down. I'll try to explain." He waited till Jimmy was settled. "You know how you can have a dream; and when you wake up, it feels like it's coming true because it's like you were awake the whole time?"

"You mean like the time I dreamed it was Christmas, and I woke up in the parlor, but it wasn't Christmas?"

He smiled. "Yeah, sort of like that." Then he became somber again. "Well, I had a bad dream the other night. In my dream I had been asleep, and when I woke up, someone had taken you. Only I didn't realize when I woke up I was still dreaming. It felt so real. Then when I really did wake up just now and saw you weren't in your bed, it felt like my dream was coming true."

"Wouldn't Daddy, I mean Mr. Pete, see if anyone tried that and catch him?"

"Yeah, most likely, but that's not the point. I was worried about you."

"I didn't think you got scared."

"I didn't say I was scared. I was worried. There's a difference."

"There is?"

Without warning, a shot rang out from just beyond the Baker property line in the woods leading to the fishing hole.

"Get down, Jimmy." Hank threw himself over his brother, shielding his body with his own as several more shots followed in rapid fire.

Chapter 16

Hank dressed quickly. "Get back in your own bed and stay here, Jimmy Jack. I don't want Ma left in the house alone. Hopefully, she's still asleep. I need to check on something."

"But…"

"Look, I'll be right back. I just want to make sure Mr. Pete's all right." He shoved his arms into his coat and grabbed his new hat from the nail. When he put it on his head, something didn't feel right. He took it off and looked at it more closely. He noticed a slight bulge in the sweatband not quite in the center of the front. "What in the world?"

"What's wrong?" Jimmy sidled up to his brother, stretching his neck to see inside the hat.

"I don't…move back." He pushed his little brother away with his elbow. "I can't see." As Hank worked to remove the object from under the leather band, it popped out and fell to the floor. It rolled briefly, and then it stopped with a plunk. "Don't move."

"What was that?"

"I'm not sure."

Hank searched all around them while they stood in place. "Did you see where it went?"

"Under your bed, I think."

They quickly dropped to their hands and knees, pushing the bedding out of the way; but it was too dark.

"Hold on. Back up. I have an idea."

Jimmy crawled backwards toward the center of their room before sitting on his haunches a few feet away. Hank lay prostrate on the floor along the length of his bed. He used his whole arm to sweep under it, using a wide arc and reaching as far back as possible. With the second returning swipe, his thumb touched something. He carefully scooted it toward him until he could grab it. He stood with what felt like a round, thick, flat object secure in his fist.

Jimmy joined him. "What is it?"

Hank opened his hand.

"It's a whittled checker painted red." He turned it over in his palm several times, admiring the crude carving of a crown on both sides.

Just then, their bedroom door opened. "I heard the gunshots. Are you boys okay?"

Hank sucked air into his lungs and quickly hid the checker under his pillow, hoping he'd been inconspicuous. "We're fine, Ma." Then he noticed her ashen face and the white knuckles of her hand on the doorknob. His heart ached for her as he sat on the edge of his mattress. "But *you're* not."

"I will be now that I know you're both all right." She played with the collar of her robe with her free hand.

Jimmy crawled back under his covers, lying on his side, and propped his head up with his fist, his elbow on his pillow. "Hank wants to make sure Da…I mean, Mr. Pete's okay."

Ma put her hands into her robe pockets as color slowly returned to her pale face.

"I'm not sure that's such a good idea. Just stay put for right now. He'll…"

Hank stood, buttoning his coat, and put his hat on his head.

"Please, Ma? I just want to make sure he's, you know, not shot."

Ma covered her mouth with her fingertips as her eyes took on a wet sheen.

Hank's shoulders slumped, his face reddening.

"Oh…don't worry. I didn't mean…. He…he's probably fine, but I don't want to assume anything. I'll be careful."

* * * * * * *

When Hank opened the barn door, the only noise and movement came from the animals in their stalls. He looked toward the hayloft, but he couldn't see anything from where he stood. It was still too dark inside. After he closed the door, he rushed to the ladder and climbed as fast as he could. He cautiously stepped onto the loft floor and looked around. He knew the mounds of hay lining the walls were as much for protection as for warmth. Mr. Pete's bedroll showed signs of having been slept in, but it was now empty, the deputy gone.

Please be all right.

Hank left the loft and checked the rest of the barn before he stepped outside and looked toward the woods. He decided to search for him there next. He knew the general direction of the shots. His familiarity with the woods between home and the river made it easy. He was pretty sure the shots had come from around the general area where he'd found Mr. Blackman's skeleton. He really didn't want to go back to the house without answers.

He secured the barn door, and then he took in a panoramic view of the property from where he stood. Satisfied all looked fine at home, he sprinted to the trailhead to his fishing hole. Once he was under the cover of the canopy in the woods, he walked down the worn path till his breathing calmed. His heart hammered against his chest, but it didn't deter him from his mission to find Mr. Pete. After a few minutes, he picked up his pace to a steady jog. Just before he reached the place where he had found the skeleton, someone clamped a hand over his mouth as his body was slammed against a hard, broad chest.

The whisper near his ear sent nerve-wracking shockwaves throughout his body. "What are you doing here, Hank? I told you to stay with your mother and brother."

It took several seconds for his mind to register the familiar voice.

Um…Granny's definitely wrong about Mr. Pete. He's a really good Indian. I never heard him…

The noise of people tramping toward them through the woods and along the trail forced them to take cover, their backs to one another behind one of the thicker pine trees. The deputy searched the woods while Hank watched the trail from where they squatted, thick brush giving them additional coverage. When he saw three men come around the bend from the direction of his fishing hole, rifles in hand and headed toward the Baker property, Hank slapped the deputy's shoulder in rapid-fire and pointed toward them. Mr. Pete pulled his weapon without cocking it. His voice was firm when he spoke to Hank.

"Stay down and wait for me right here, do you understand?"

"Yes, sir."

The deputy moved quickly and quietly, back-tracking their position. Within a few seconds, Hank watched Mr. Pete meet up with the men and holster his gun. He tried to listen to their conversation, but they were too far away and talked too softly. From the deputy's relaxed gestures and seemingly cordial manner with them, Hank guessed he knew the men. He felt his own nerves relax and began to mimic Mr. Pete's behavior.

Just then, another shot rang out from the river, farther down the trail from where they were. The group dispersed. Hank watched the deputy move toward him with what seemed like superhuman speed.

"You can show yourself now, son."

Hank stood where he had been squatting, his cramped muscles resisting the change with excruciating pain. His body froze, mesmerized by Mr. Pete's appearance. The man's eyes flashed with heat, his face red under streaks of war paint.

Whoa! How did I miss seeing that *until just now? He* looks *like an Indian!*

The deputy put heavy hands on Hank's shoulders, his fingers digging into his flesh. There was an intensity in the man's eyes Hank had not seen since the incident with the Ku Klux Klan. "What are you doing out here? This is police business, Hank. I'm on the job. I need you to go back to the house. I don't want to have to worry about you while we're tracking this fugitive. Do you understand?"

Hank nodded, unable to stop looking at the transformation he saw in the deputy's appearance. "Yes, sir."

"Please go home and wait for me to return. It shouldn't be long now."

"Yes, sir."

Before Hank could leave, Mr. Pete crushed him in a strong bear hug. One of his big hands cupped the back of Hank's head while the man's chin rested on the crown of his head. "I could never have forgiven myself, son, if anything had happened to you. Please don't scare me like this again. I love you like you were my own, but you have to understand my position here. This situation is *my* responsibility, not yours. It's police business. Let *me* handle it."

As if they had minds of their own, Hank's arms wrapped around Mr. Pete's waist and squeezed for what seemed like a full minute before he let the man go.

"Yes, sir."

* * * * * * *

As Hank made his way home, he pondered Mr. Pete's words and actions just now. When he put them together with what the deputy had shared in the meeting with the pastor, he felt a wellspring of warmth flood his body. Slowly, he realized some of the weight he had carried while his daddy was gone had lifted. *We're safe with him, Daddy. You can...* Hank swallowed past a lump in his throat and blinked away tears threatening to fall over his cheeks. *You can rest in peace.*

The smell of coffee blended with bacon in the frying pan and biscuits right from the oven as Hank climbed the back porch steps. The aromas welcomed him when he opened the back door and watched Jimmy finish setting the table for four. Ma looked at him from the stove as he shut the door and shrugged out of his coat. Her eyes were still bright with unshed tears.

"Did you find him?"

"Yes, ma'am, he's all right."

Her face brightened for a moment. "You saw him?"

"Yes, ma'am, he was headed into the woods with some men he knew. He didn't say anything to me specifically, but I think they've found Mr. Higgins. He's close, Ma."

She nodded and turned her attention back to her morning routine. Hank overheard her soft prayer as he joined her at the sink. "Keep him safe, Lord."

"Do you want us to do the chores now or wait?"

She washed and dried her hands before moving to the stove. "They need to be done, but..." She paused momentarily before pouring uncooked grits into the pot of boiling water. "I tell you what. Why don't you at least start them now, but keep watch for anyone coming out of the woods. I want you to get back to the house quickly if you see anyone or hear any more shots."

"Yes, ma'am; come on, Jimmy. You take care of the henhouse; I'll take care of the barn. That way, the eggs are collected and the livestock's fed at least. The rest can wait till Mr. Pete gets back."

"That's good, son. Do that, but do it quickly. I don't want you out there any longer than necessary while he's gone."

"Yes, ma'am."

* * * * * * *

Hank put the livestock in the corral to feed them, thinking it would be best to put them out to pasture after Mr. Pete came home. *Home...hmmm...may as well get used to it. It'll be his home before long, anyway.*

As he mucked the stalls, Hank thought about the meeting he needed to have with Daniel, Beth Ann, and Abraham. *I just hope they'll come over today.* He was concerned about missing school, and not because of the extra homework. There was no way to get word to Daniel or Beth Ann about what was happening. At least they had all agreed the fishing hole was not safe right now.

He didn't want to put any of his friends in danger, but he knew they could help him decipher what he knew. He also needed their combined talents to figure out what to do with the information he had. Until then, he really didn't know if he had anything significant to tell Mr. Pete or not. *I don't want to worry him unnecessarily.* The memory of what had happened in the woods earlier was still fresh in his mind, stirring emotions he couldn't remember having before that very moment.

Suddenly, his mind flashed to the checker he'd found in his hat. The nerves around his hairline sparked. He automatically rubbed the nape of his neck. *Someone had to have put it there intentionally.* He figured Uncle Will was somehow involved because of the note, but what does it have to do with anything else?

Just as he finished his chores, he noticed someone walk out of the woods from the familiar trail he often used. He looked behind him in the direction of the chicken yard.

"Jimmy, get in the house." He watched his brother set the feed bucket aside and grab the egg basket without hesitation, and then he watched him head toward the back porch.

Once his brother was safely inside, Hank hid behind the cistern at the side of the barn undetected, he hoped, and watched. At first, he didn't recognize who deliberately, but unhurriedly, crossed the Baker field. It was obvious the man headed straight for the house, though. Hank's heart beat wildly. His mind shouted for him to go inside like Ma had told him to do if he saw anyone, but his feet wouldn't obey. Then he noticed the man's painted face. *Mr. Pete!*

Hank stepped away from his hiding place and kept his focus on the deputy while walking along the outside of the corral, pacing himself so as to converge with Mr. Pete in the yard near the pump. The closer they got to one another, the more defined the man's facial expression became. Hank's heart skipped a couple of beats as he recognized the look of indignation in his deportment.

When he thought about their earlier encounter more carefully, there was definitely something amiss even then. As they approached one another's position, they slowed as if in sync with each other's thoughts and purposes. Hank saw fatigue replace whatever had been Mr. Pete's demeanor before, but there was no satisfaction or relief detected in the man's behavior.

"Mr. Pete, you don't look so good. Did they get him? Mr. Higgins, I mean."

Before the deputy answered, he pumped water and splashed his face several times, using his shirt to remove the war paint. "Are your chores finished?"

"Yes, sir, the ones Ma told us to do before you got home."

"Good. Let's eat, and then let me get cleaned up. We need to talk."

"Yes, sir. It's bad, isn't it?"

Mr. Pete sighed and looked around the property. "Yeah, son, it is."

Chapter 17

Hank sat at the kitchen table, his hands clasped tightly together in his lap. His knees quivered with jittery nerves as he waited for the deputy to speak. Ma did laundry in the wash house while Jimmy played on the tire swing hanging from the sweet gum tree near the driveway. Hank was glad Mr. Pete had asked Ma to let them talk alone.

It had taken nearly an hour for this meeting to finally happen. After breakfast, the deputy went home to clean up and had just returned in uniform, officially on duty for the day. Hank felt as if he were in the principal's office. He was determined to remain silent until necessary, for fear of getting into more trouble if he said anything.

Surely they found Mr. Higgins.

He watched the deputy pour himself a fresh cup of coffee at the stove.

Is he on his way back to jail? If he is, then why isn't Mr. Pete more relieved? Instead, he seems...doggone it...I wish I could read his face better.

The longer Mr. Pete avoided looking at Hank, the faster his knees bounced. When the deputy finally took a seat across from him, the man placed his elbows on the table and crossed his arms between them.

I think he's trying to relax, but why? What could have happened out there in the woods this morning?

Deputy Collins stared at a spot on the tablecloth for what seemed like hours to Hank. Worry lines spread across the man's forehead. Then he opened and shut his mouth a couple of times as he scowled.

Hank swallowed past a lump in his throat. *Come on, Mr. Pete. You're scaring me more than the idea that Mr. Higgins is still on the loose.*

Then the deputy blew out a long breath and looked directly at Hank. His eyes showed kindness, but they also looked sad.

"I've been trying to figure out how to tell you…but…well…." Mr. Pete shook his head a couple of times. "There's just no easy way to talk about this, son." He paused for several more agonizing seconds, blinking fast as he looked at the ceiling briefly.

"Mr. Pete, it's okay." Hank shrugged his shoulders. "I'd rather hear it from you than not know."

The deputy nodded and took a sip of his coffee. "I can definitely relate to that and respect you for it. However…I wish you didn't have to go through any of this at all, if you want to know the truth. I don't want you to feel like you're to blame…for *any* of it. You've already lost so much of your childhood innocence, what with everything you've had to deal with. But…."

"But I handled it, didn't I?"

"Yes, you did, and very well, I might add. It's just that no kid should ever have to…"

"Look, my daddy used to tell me life is never supposed to be easy. It's about learning from mistakes and getting through the hard times better at the end than when they began. He also told me he couldn't protect me from everything, no matter how hard he wanted to. I'm thinking this is one of those times you'll have to trust me to get through on my own."

Mr. Pete grinned. "He's right, and so are you. But you're not by yourself, Hank. I want you to know I'm here to stand with you since he can't. I'll do what I can when it's appropriate. "

"If I didn't believe that, I wouldn't be okay with you marrying Ma."

The deputy's lopsided smile relieved some of Hank's uneasiness. "You have a point." Then the frown returned. Deputy Collins ran his fingers through his thick, dark hair as he blew out a hard sigh. He took another sip of coffee and nodded. "Okay, then, here's what you need to know." He sat back in his chair. Then he stretched out his arms in front of him and wrapped his hands around his coffee cup. He looked directly into Hank's eyes while he spoke.

"The men you saw with me this morning were from the Camden police force. Several deputies from the posse were following a blood trail they were pretty sure belonged to the man they tracked from Cullendale. The last shot we heard was their signal. They'd found him."

"Was it Mr. Higgins? Had they shot him?"

The deputy nodded. "Yeah, it was." Then he shook his head. "And no, they hadn't."

Hank sat up, relief washing over him. "Is he back in jail?"

"No, he's…he's at Doc Warden's clinic. I'll be meeting the sheriff there when I leave here."

Hank slumped in his chair, trying hard to keep dread from overtaking his ability to think. "But…they caught him. That's good, isn't it? I mean, he can't hurt me now, right?"

Mr. Pete bowed his head briefly before looking up again. "No, son, he can't, but there's more. His wounds…well…he lost a lot of blood. He's dying."

"Dying? But…" Hank swallowed bitter spit, and then he realized why he respected Mr. Pete so much. He valued life, no matter whose it was.

"We're hoping he'll be able to answer some questions before he…"

"It's over, isn't it?"

"Well, that's the thing. Before he passed out, he gave the deputy who found him some information. But he spoke nonsense, possibly being cryptic. Do you know what that means?"

"I think so. It means he used a code to pass on a hidden message, or something like that."

The deputy smiled as he nodded. "Very good." Then his smile faded. "We think there's something more going on than anyone thought possible. According to the deputy, Mr. Higgins was more interested in your safety than getting even with you. That's why he escaped…to warn you. But what he said next causes all of us grave concern."

Hank's heart skipped a beat, and every nerve sparked.

"Are you saying I'm still in danger?"

Mr. Pete looked out the kitchen window before making eye contact with Hank again, shaking his head and shrugging his shoulders slightly. "I don't think so, but I'm really not a hundred percent sure. That's why…"

Hank felt the blood drain from his face.

The deputy leaned forward a bit and clasped his hands, his facial expression the same as when they began this conversation. "I need to ask you something. Don't take it personally…just humor me, okay?"

Hank nodded.

"Is it possible you inadvertently left out *anything* when you told me about your kidnapping or what led up to it?"

Hank's mind replayed the events connected with that day. "No, sir, I told you everything."

"Just to be sure, will you tell me about it again?"

"Okay, I was on my way home from the river after fishing. I hadn't gone far on the trail when someone hit me on the back of my head, and I blacked out. The next thing I remember is waking up alone in a shed. It was dark inside, but not outside. There was sunlight coming in from between the boards used for the walls. I wasn't sure how long I had been out or where I was, so I didn't know whether it was sunset or sunrise. I knew it could have been either. When I tried to sit up, I felt like I was going to throw up. And my head hurt really badly. I was dizzy every now and then, and I saw stars sometimes." Hank suppressed a chill and licked his lips.

"Did you hear anything before you were hit?"

"No, sir, I don't think so…maybe, but I'm not sure."

"That's okay; do you remember what you were thinking?"

"No, sir, not really."

"Not a problem. You're doing fine. What happened next?"

"I tried to find out where I was by peeking through the space between the boards, but I didn't recognize anything. Then someone brought me food, but he didn't let me go. I couldn't eat much, but I do remember it didn't taste good, not like Ma's cooking."

Mr. Pete chuckled. "I agree. Your ma's a *great* cook." Immediately, Hank felt tension leave his body, and he grinned. His shoulder and back muscles relaxed a bit, even though the mood quickly switched back to being serious. "Sorry for the digression. Go on with your account."

"That's all right. I think we both needed to laugh a little." Hank rolled his neck and shoulders before continuing. "Not long after that, Uncle Will took me inside the cabin where two men were waiting. One of the men, Mr. Higgins, wanted to know where I had hidden the whiskey I had stolen from him. I figured he was the leader by the way he was acting. He was the one Mr. Sawyer and Uncle Will talked about when I spied on them. I was behind a nearby tree when they mentioned him by name. They were right over the place where they had buried the whiskey on our land. Anyway, when I wouldn't tell him what he wanted to know, he threatened to torture it out of me. You know the rest. You were listening outside before you came in."

"You didn't see anyone else besides Higgins, Sawyer, and your uncle?"

"No, sir."

"Did they mention any other names?"

Hank thought for several seconds before speaking, and then shook his head. "No, sir, but I kind of got the feeling there was something not right about the way they were acting. I couldn't understand why they were so concerned over one box of moonshine whiskey when it's so easy to get."

"Tell me about the whiskey you buried."

Hank scratched his head, and then shifted in his chair before placing his folded hands on top of the table. "Well, as soon as I knew Uncle Will and Mr. Sawyer were really gone, I dug up the box. It was a wooden crate, but it was too heavy for me to lift out of the hole by myself. So I pried open the lid and looked inside before I decided what to do. There were twelve bottles in all."

"Good…wait…" Mr. Pete's brows came together in a scowl, but his voice wasn't angry when he finally spoke. "You're sure you found bottles? Not jars or jugs?"

"Yes, sir."

"Can you remember seeing a label on the bottles?"

"Maybe, but I don't really remember. I was more interested in getting rid of them."

"Okay, go ahead. What did you do after you found the bottles?"

"I found a place away from their hole and farther down the trail between our place and Granny Rose's. I decided to dig a deeper hole away from the trail itself and bury the bottles in it so no one could ever find them. It was so obvious where *they* had buried it. But I didn't want Ma to be in trouble with the G-men. You remember the agents who were here during that time?"

Mr. Pete nodded and sat up a bit taller in his chair.

Hank matched the deputy's posture. "I made sure my hiding place was impossible to find. I didn't want Granny in trouble, either. When I figured the new hole was big enough, I took three or four bottles at a time and laid them in it. I didn't care if they broke or leaked. I just knew I didn't want to pour out the stuff and have it stink up our property. I figured that would've made the G-men stay around longer."

The deputy smiled and nodded, his face more relaxed.

"When I put the last bottle in the hole, I refilled it and made sure the ground on top was as flat as before. I also put leaves and brush over it so it didn't look different from the rest of the area from the trail. Then I put the lid back on the empty crate in the original hole and buried it again, leaving a mound like they had so it looked undisturbed."

"I'm impressed. You did good, son. Do you remember where you buried the bottles?"

"Not really. I didn't *want* to remember. I intentionally made it look so much like it did when I saw the place even *I* wouldn't be able to find it. As far as I'm concerned, it's gone and can stay lost forever."

Mr. Pete smiled and shook his head as he became serious again. "That's it? There's nothing else?"

"No, sir, that's it." Then Hank remembered the notes. He resisted rubbing the back of his neck.

"Okay, just a couple more questions. Do you know who dug up the crate after you buried it?"

"No, sir. I assume it was Uncle Will or Mr. Sawyer. From the conversation I overheard, Mr. Higgins didn't know that it was buried, much less where. As far as I know, no one else knew anything about it, either."

"Would you show me where it was buried?"

"I'll try."

"That's all I can ask. I'll say this, though. Whether we find it or not, son, I'm proud of you and how you handled yourself."

Hank felt his ears get hot. "Thanks."

Mr. Pete looked at his pocket watch. "All right, I need to go for now. The sheriff is waiting for me at the clinic. Stay close to home today. Hopefully, things will be back to normal in a couple of days. Then we'll look for the crate."

"Yes, sir."

* * * * * * *

Before Mr. Pete left, he and Ma talked as she hung clothes from a basket on the line nearest the wash house. While they talked, Hank and Jimmy took turns swinging on the tire swing. At one point, Jimmy swung in the opening while Hank was on top of the tire.

"Hey, stop. We're too heavy together. What if we take turns standing here. Then we can push each other and see how high we can get and how far we can jump. Let me get down before you climb up here, and I'll push you first. Then you can push me."

Jimmy's face lit up with a broad smile. "Why didn't we think of that before?"

"I don't know. Sometimes, we have to do things the hard way to realize there's a better way."

Everything went as planned, and the brothers laughed and jumped and laughed some more. Hank was on his fourth time on the tire when he heard something different from the usual creaks and moans from the rope. He looked up at the limb and then at the knot in the rope. Nothing appeared to be wrong, so he continued swinging. Aiding Jimmy's pushes, he used his legs to propel himself even higher. When he finally reached the height he wanted, he took a flying leap. His landing was perfect by his estimation, with a roll-out to soften the jarring blow to his legs when he hit the ground.

Jimmy clapped his hands. "Woo-hoo! That was the best one so far. It's my turn, now."

"Sure, come on. Let me help you up first." Hank held the tire still while his brother climbed into position. "Here goes, now. Hang on tight, and don't forget to let me know when to get out of the way so you can jump."

"Okay, let's go."

Hank pulled the tire toward him and pushed it till the momentum was steady. Then he held onto the tire as he ran under it, adding more altitude to Jimmy's eventual launch. As Hank ran around to duplicate the action, he heard a snap overhead and watched the rope break into two pieces. Immediately, everything went into slow motion as he heard his brother scream and watched him sail through the air until he plummeted to the ground with a crunch and an echoing POP! Jimmy lay still where he landed in a heap, his left leg lay in an unnatural angle away from his small body.

Hank's heart hurt as it pounded against his chest. "Jimmy! Ma! Mr. Pete!"

Chapter 18

Time stood still for Hank. While he sat in the waiting room at the clinic, he replayed the accident over and over in his mind, trying to will it to end differently. His little brother's leg was broken in two places. Dr. Warden couldn't do anything for him, so he prepared Jimmy for the drive to Camden. He needed surgery to set the bones.

The drama playing out before Hank seemed surreal. It felt like forever ago since they had arrived to get his brother the medical attention he needed. They were all glad he was still unconscious, but now there was cause for concern. Hank heard the adults' words and understood some of what was being said. But it was like he was moving through a fog and observing everything from a distance.

No...this can't be happening! Now they're talking about brain damage, God, as if his broken leg weren't enough! Thanks a lot! What are you doing to me?

Without saying anything to anyone, Hank walked out of the clinic and toward the church. So far, he'd been able to keep his wits, but the numbness was wearing off. As his mind continued to flash scenes from the horrible accident, a dark, oppressive guilt came over him. When the cemetery came into view, he ran hard and fast till he arrived at the closed gate.

He fumbled with the latch unsuccessfully. Tears streamed down his face as anger drove him to growl and groan out of frustration. He eventually climbed the fence and ran to his daddy's grave, where he collapsed on top of the seasoned dirt mound. His sobs hurt his sides.

It's my fault, Daddy. It's all my fault Jimmy's hurt. I've failed you. I didn't keep him safe. Now he's hurt really bad. I'm afraid he'll lose his leg because of me. I'm so sorry, Daddy. I'm so sorry.

"Hank, son..."

Hank instantly sat up and looked at the tombstone, shocked to finally hear the familiar voice after weeks of silence. His heart skipped a beat. "Daddy?"

Someone put a hand on Hank's shoulder from behind. He jumped and turned around. Mr. Pete knelt behind him, tears in his eyes, too. "Please don't blame yourself for what happened this morning."

Hey...the voice...it wasn't...? I thought...wait...how'd Mr. Pete know...? I didn't say those things out loud...did I?

"It was an accident. No one blames you, certainly not me or your mother. Please hear me. *It was an accident,* that's all."

"But..."

The deputy shook his head. "No, son. No 'buts.' You are *not* at fault."

"What's going to happen to him?"

"Doc called ahead. There's a doctor, a surgeon, waiting for Jimmy to arrive at the hospital. He'll have to be there for a while to make sure he's healing properly. Then he'll come home, and we'll take him back for checkups."

Hank fell limp onto the deputy's chest and sobbed some more. "Mr. Pete, I let Daddy down. I promised to take care of our family, but I failed. I let Jimmy get hurt, badly this time. What if he loses his leg?"

The deputy embraced him with a tight squeeze, and then he rubbed Hank's back. "Son, you're borrowing worries from a future we can't possibly know. Listen to yourself. You're being unreasonable. Do you honestly think your father would blame you for this accident?"

Hank squeezed his eyes shut as more tears trailed down his cheeks unchecked, soaking the front of Mr. Pete's shirt. After several seconds, he sat up and shook his head, unable to look at the man's face. "I don't know."

The deputy cupped Hank's shoulders with his big, warm hands. "Hey, look at me." He waited for Hank to comply. "I'm telling you he wouldn't. He couldn't. You've done nothing wrong. You've done nothing to be ashamed of, either. You did everything right. You got your brother help quickly and probably saved his leg *and* his life. Don't let anyone, not even yourself, tell you differently. You're a hero today, son. Your dad would be proud. I know I am."

Hank wiped his face with his sleeves, needing to blow his nose badly. "You mean it?"

Mr. Pete smiled. "Yes, I do. Now, come on. Your mom needs to leave with Jimmy, but she didn't want to go without seeing you first. Here, take this and make yourself presentable so she doesn't worry about you." The deputy handed Hank his handkerchief.

Hank wiped his cheeks and eyes before he blew his nose, and then the deputy helped him up.

"Stand tall, now. Your mom's waiting for us."

"Yes, sir." He breathed in a ragged breath and let it out slowly.

"May I ask you something?"

Hank nodded, fighting to keep his composure.

"Would it be okay if I stayed with you while your mom and Jimmy are in Camden? We can keep each other company while they're away. Just don't be surprised if I'm there for a couple of weeks, if not longer."

"Sure." Hank's lips quivered as he nodded, and then he wiped at his eyes again. "Actually, I'd really like that…a lot."

"Good. We thought it would be best if your ma stayed with Jimmy till he came home. But I didn't want you to be alone. Besides, what better way to *really* get to know one another than spending time together, just the two of us?"

"Okay."

"We'll need to pack a bag for your mom, and then take it to her. Are you up for that?"

"Yes, sir, but…well, what about Mr. Higgins?"

"The sheriff's taking care of that till I've taken care of this. Family has to come first in this kind of situation. My job will always be there when the crisis is over. So don't go adding that to your worry list, you hear?"

Hank nodded. "Yes, sir."

"You know, you need to learn how to be a kid. Do you think Daniel would be willing to take that job?"

They both smiled. "Probably. He told me the same thing on Saturday."

"He's a smart kid, and he's a great friend. But seriously, you're not alone with your family anymore, son. I'm here for all three of you from now on. How about it, will you let me take that burden off your shoulders?"

"I'll try."

"We'll work on it together, okay?"

"Yes, sir, I'd like that, too."

* * * * * * *

Hank couldn't believe it was only a few minutes after one in the afternoon when Mr. Pete turned his motorcar onto the Baker property. His stomach growled, but he really wasn't hungry. Even though he hadn't eaten since breakfast, he wasn't sure he could keep anything down anyway. His nerves were still raw. As they parked under the sweet gum tree, Hank stared at the tire on the grass across the way. It still lay where it had fallen.

"When we get back from Camden, we'll take care of that. Meanwhile, don't let guilt rob you of the good you've done today, okay?"

"It's hard."

"But not impossible. Let's get your mom's bag packed."

"Yes, sir."

Neither spoke while they moved about the house. As they prepared to leave, Hank looked at the clothesline. "What about the laundry?"

"Well, your mom was hanging the last basketful when the accident happened. I think she had finished it. As far as I know, all that's left to do is to take them off the line when they're dry. When she and Jimmy are settled at the hospital, I'll bring you back here and go back to work. Check on the clothes then, and take care of them for her, okay?"

Hank nodded. "Sure." He settled into the front seat of the sedan again. The noise of the engine lulled him into taking a short nap. Just as he closed his eyes to let sleep come, he thought about the meeting he had set up for later in the afternoon with his friends. He looked over at Mr. Pete. "Will it be okay if Daniel and Beth Ann come over after school?"

"I think that's a good idea. Then you won't be here by yourself for too long before I'm off duty. Just don't leave the farm while they're here, okay?"

"What about Abraham? We've kind of planned to meet up with him, too."

"All right, but I'd still rather you stay home. Don't go fishing. As for Abraham, what about this? I'll go over to Granny's after I drop you off and tell him to come over when he's finished with his work?"

"Okay, thanks." After several yawns and a couple of attempts to sleep, Hank decided to watch the scenery instead. He stared out the side window as they made their way to town. He worked at blocking all thought processes, so worry wouldn't take hold and mock his efforts to accept the truth of all that had happened since Friday.

* * * * * * *

When Mr. Pete and Hank arrived at the county hospital in Camden, Jimmy had already been in surgery for almost half an hour. They found Ma in the room where they would stay while the doctors monitored his recovery. Both Beth Ann's and Daniel's moms were with her, along with a couple of ladies from the church. Pastor Bob and his wife, Miss Tootsie, were there, too. Each of them looked at Hank with compassion and smiles. They all told him he'd done well, but his mind still warred against the guilt niggling on the edge of his fragile heart.

The surgery took a little more than a couple of hours. A short while afterwards, they all learned Jimmy was resting comfortably. However, the surgeon told Ma and Mr. Pete the next twenty-four hours would be critical for determining his recovery. There was still the danger of infection, which could warrant the decision to save his life by amputating the injured leg. Hank's heart ached. His breathing became fast and shallow as he considered the actuality of the worst case scenario. The room spun as he registered the doctor's words in his overactive mind.

"Are you all right, son?" Hank turned at the sound of Ma's soft voice. She and Mr. Pete sat on either side of him. She smoothed his hair from his forehead. "You're going to need a haircut soon."

"I'm scared, Ma. What if…"

The deputy put a hand on Hank's shoulder while Ma held one of his hands and gently squeezed. "Don't you do that to yourself, Hank. We're not going to think about the 'what ifs' at all. Honey,

Dr. Nelson said your brother came through the operation just fine. Didn't you hear him say that? I believe if he were really concerned about major complications, he would have warned us."

"But what he said, Ma...what about the next twenty-four hours?"

Mr. Pete patted his shoulder. "Hey, don't go there, either. All surgery has its risks. Everyone who has an operation has to be watched carefully for the first twenty-four hours afterwards. It's routine. His comment is a basic reminder so the family doesn't overlook the potential for fever or infection or any number of other issues that *can* happen to change the outcome. It doesn't mean it *will* happen."

"Pete, why don't you two go on home? There's nothing else you can do here. The doctor wants Jimmy to sleep today, so his leg has the best chance to heal. If anything happens, I'll call Dr. Warden so he can get word to you. Jimmy's in God's hands. I have complete peace about his recovery." Ma kissed Hank's temple. "Go home, now, and rest yourselves. Come back tomorrow, and you'll see I'm right. Everything's going to be back to normal before we all know it."

For the first time, Hank noticed how tired Ma looked, but her face had a glow about it he couldn't explain. *Is that the peace she talked about, God? Why won't you give me some of it?*

* * * * * * *

It was mid-afternoon when the deputy and Hank headed back to Farmville. Before they left the hospital, the church ladies assured them they would start a prayer vigil and keep it going until they knew Jimmy was awake and on the mend. They also promised to bring food by starting tomorrow morning and keep it coming for as long as the family needed it. As Mr. Pete drove in silence, Hank pondered the conversations he'd had with him and Ma. He desperately tried to draw encouragement and strength from them.

He also thought about the way their friends and community had, once again, shown their love and concern for his family. The last time they'd done so was for his daddy's funeral. Hank was so glad they weren't here because of another death, although he knew how easily it could have been. He yawned several times, struggling to stay awake.

"When we get to the house, why don't you take a nap? You look tired."

"Yes, sir, I am. What time is it, anyway?"

The deputy pulled his watch from his trousers pocket and opened it. "It's about ten minutes after three o'clock."

"It feels like it ought to be a lot later."

"Yeah, time seems to go slower when we're dealing with trauma. I think it's the body's way of coping with it."

Neither spoke again for several minutes, not until they pulled into the driveway and parked.

"Hey, everything's going to be fine, okay? I'll try to be back before dark, but I have several things I need to take care of before I can leave the office. Why don't you walk over to Granny's with Abraham? I told Miss Tootsie we'd have supper with her tonight. We'll come back here to sleep. Just be sure to take care of your chores before leaving, okay?"

He yawned again while nodding. "Yes, sir, I'll do that."

Hank got out of the car and walked up to the porch. The deputy didn't leave until he went in. He watched Mr. Pete drive away, and then he remembered the laundry. When he brought the clothes in from the line, he put them in Ma's bedroom, and then he went to his own room. He lay on his back on top of his covers and draped one arm over his eyes, but sleep was the farthest thing from his mind. As sleepy as he had been on the drive home, he was now wide awake. The grandfather clock in the parlor struck half past three.

I may as well get up. Besides, Daniel and Beth Ann will be here before long.

When Hank went outside, his eyes automatically went to the tire lying on the grass just beyond the driveway. His stomach churned with nausea as he stared at the fallen swing. He swallowed past the lump in his throat as his eyes looked at the frayed rope still hanging from the limb. Something looked odd, but he couldn't quite figure out what. So he dismissed it for the moment and walked over to the tire on the ground.

As he set the tire on its end and rolled it toward the tree, he heard a rattling sound inside the wheel well of thick rubber. Before he leaned it against the rough bark of the trunk, he tried to look for the object in question; but it was too dark. He reached his hand inside the hollow tire and groped for several seconds until his fingers touched something bumpy, flat, and round. When he finally grasped it, he pulled it out and felt his hair bristle around the nape of his neck.

A red checker! Just like the one from my hat!

He raced to his room and dropped to his knees in front of his nightstand. He couldn't tell if his heavy breathing was because he'd run or from fear. He slowly opened the drawer and looked inside. *It's still here.* He grabbed the checker he'd found in his hat and compared it with the one in his other hand from the tire. They were identical.

What in the world?

Just then, Hank heard distant voices from the road near the end of the driveway. He put both checkers in his trousers pocket, and then looked out his window. He saw Daniel and Beth Ann coming up the drive. They each had a long tree limb they used for walking sticks. He grinned when he saw them use them like swords at one point.

As he stepped out onto the porch, they hailed him and ran the rest of the way, meeting him under the place where the tire swing used to hang. The two runners slowed as they approached the tree. Hank noticed them looking up at the same time. From the puzzled expressions on their faces, he knew they had noticed the dangling rope piece still attached to the limb. Then they shifted their attention to him.

Daniel pointed at the tire with his walking stick. "What happened to the swing?"

Hank swallowed past another wave of nausea and sadness before he answered. "There was an accident this morning while Jimmy and I were taking turns swinging. It broke while he was on it. He's in the hospital in Camden."

Beth Ann's face paled. "What? I wondered why my dad was glad I was coming over and asked me to check on you. He said there'd been an accident, but he couldn't go into details because he was in the middle of another emergency. I could tell today's been a tough one for him. When I saw you were okay, I just assumed he'd made a mistake. I'm really sorry. Is he going to be all right?"

"Yeah, but he broke his leg in two places and had to have surgery."

"Was that why you weren't at school today?"

"No, Mr. Pete got some news about the prisoner they were looking for and wanted us to stay close to home."

Daniel's voice cracked. "What do you mean 'were' looking for? You said, 'were looking for.'"

"Yeah, it's kind of a long story. Let's wait till Abraham gets here before I tell it."

Beth Ann looked toward the tire, and then walked over to it. She squatted to get a closer look. She picked up the end of the rope, and they watched her run her fingers over the frayed edges. Then she slowly twirled it back and forth between her thumb and fingers. "Hey, did you see this?"

Hank knelt beside her as Daniel leaned over their shoulders.

"It looks like part of this rope was cut, maybe a quarter of an inch at least. See how these strands have clean edges?" She pointed to the ragged end of the rope. "The rest of it has stretched and uneven edges. Your weight pulled it apart because it was too weak to hold you without the part that's cut. Add to that the weight of another person and the swinging motion, and it's a disaster waiting to happen."

"She's right, Hank. You need to show this to Deputy Collins. Is he here?"

Hank took the rope from Beth Ann and looked closely at the edges. Then he smelled it. "Not now, but he *will* be later. He's staying with me while Ma and Jimmy are in Camden."

Beth Ann wiped her hands on her overalls legs before standing. "If you ask me, I'd say this was no accident. Do you agree, Daniel?"

"Yeah, I do." Daniel nodded and joined her. "Do you think it's because you didn't meet the deadline?"

"What deadline?"

Hank felt the blood drain from his face as he stood with his friends. "Maybe, but I don't know."

"What deadline, Hank?"

"I'll explain when Abraham gets here." He thought about the checkers in his pocket, and then he pulled them out. "What do you two think about these?"

As soon as he opened his hands to show them the checkers, Beth Ann gasped. "I've seen those before. Well, not those exact ones, but some like them. A man came to the clinic on Saturday and had a red one and a black one. I saw them when he emptied his pockets to get money out to pay for some bandages. When he saw me looking at them, he quickly put them back in his pocket. He kept looking at me with the most hateful glare. I'm telling you, he actually gave me the creeps. You two know me. That doesn't happen often, but I was definitely glad when he left."

Daniel took the checkers from Hank's hand and scowled as he turned them over in his own hand. "They look homemade. Where'd you get them?"

"One was in my new hat. Remember me telling you it was missing? When we got back from Smackover, it was on my bed.

The checker was in the sweatband under the rim. I found the other one in the tire just before you got here."

"Okay, you two have some explaining to do. I'm feeling a bit left out of this, and I don't like it at all."

"I'm sorry, Beth Ann. I'll tell you everything I've already told Daniel and more when Abraham gets here."

"You'd better. I'm holding you to it."

Daniel smiled. "I told you she'd react like that."

Hank grinned. "Yeah, you were right."

His friend held the checkers in his open palm so they could all see them. "What do you suppose they mean?"

Beth Ann shook her head as she took one and turned it over in her own hand. "My guess is nothing good. I got a really bad feeling from that man in the clinic."

Hank took the other and examined it more closely in the sunlight. "I think it's probably a warning of some kind because there was a note with the one in my hat."

"Are you talking about the note with the deadline, or was it a third one?"

Beth Ann sighed. "Oh, come on, guys. There's more than one note? You're killing me, here."

"No, it was the one with the deadline, but I didn't think the two were connected. Now I'm thinking I was wrong. It seems like too much of a coincidence. Say, what time of the day was that man at the clinic on Saturday, Beth Ann?"

"Hmmm, let me think." She paused for several seconds. "I think...yeah, it was my dad's last patient before we closed for lunch. Why?"

Hank nodded.

"Well, that..."

Daniel came to the same conclusion at the exact same time as Hank.

"Do you think he's the one who was in your house on Saturday?"

Beth Ann crossed her arms over her chest. "Your house was broken into while you were in Smackover? Just what else haven't you told me?"

"I don't know, but maybe. Beth Ann, I promise to fill you in on everything when…"

"Yeah, yeah, when Abraham gets here…I get it. Just don't expect me to be happy about waiting. You're going to owe me big time for this, buster."

"I understand, and I don't blame you for being upset. I'd probably feel the same way. But for now, I need you to think. Do you remember what the man you're talking about looked like? I take it he wasn't from around here or you would have called him by name."

She looked as if she were looking for something in the tree branches behind Hank. Her eyes squinted, then she looked directly at him, nodding. "Yeah, I think so."

"Good. Because I want you to tell Mr. Pete about him. If this rope was cut, he could have done it. And if it *wasn't* an accident, I may have been the one who was supposed to get hurt, not Jimmy."

Chapter 19

Hank felt safer under the sweet gum tree than in the hayloft when Abraham arrived. So they all sat in a circle on the grass across the driveway from where Jimmy fell. The gravity of Hank's circumstances struck some dire chords on his nerves, bringing a morbid sense of reality to the whole situation. Anxiety, fear, and paranoia fought together to wrestle control away from being level headed, calm, and sane.

Now if someone comes onto our property, I'll know because I can see better from here.

He relayed all he had shared with Daniel on the way back from Smackover, and the most recent events as soon as everyone was settled. With answering questions along the way, it took most of an hour to tell them everything. The more he told them, though, the queasier his stomach felt, especially when he considered Jimmy's accident to be a failed attempt on his own life. It changed the dynamics of the status of things as they knew them to be.

"Look, it helps to talk about all of this with you three, but I have to be honest. I'm really nervous about getting you involved. I think it's obvious I'm a target. That makes me dangerous to be around. Just look at what happened to my little brother."

The protests came at once from all three of Hank's closest friends. It made his heart feel warm, but the pit of his stomach felt as if there were pins and needles sticking him from the inside out.

Beth Ann jabbed his knee several times with her index finger, her face red and her brows furrowed. "Don't even *think* about shutting us out."

Hank's emotions broke a dam deep in his gut. Tears overflowed his eyes and rolled down his cheeks unrestrained. "I don't want anyone else hurt because of what I did this summer. Maybe we just need to let Mr. Pete and Sheriff Stan handle this one. Jimmy could have been killed this morning." He angrily wiped at his face with the backs of his hands, his own brows furrowed. "If I hadn't gotten involved…"

Abraham put his hand on Hank's shoulder. "I would probably be dead, to say nothing about Granny or my mammy or the others you've helped."

Beth Ann leaned across the space in front of Hank and put her hand on one of his knees. Worry lines creased her forehead, but her anger was obviously gone. "Listen to him. He's right. You got involved because you care."

Daniel covered Hank's other shoulder with his hand. "Do you remember how your dad was described at his funeral?" Hank sniffed, and then he wiped his nose on his sleeve. "Yeah, so what?"

"So what? Hank, they may as well have been describing you. When you put this team together this summer, do you realize what you did?"

He shook his head without looking up at anyone. "No, aside from putting you all in danger for my own selfish reasons, I don't…not exactly."

"You gave us a mission in life. Do you know what that means?" Hank looked at Daniel briefly. "I never thought about what I was good at until you pointed it out to me. I really am learning something from reading those Sherlock Holmes stories, and I *like* it. Then there's Beth Ann. You've never questioned her desire to be a doctor, even though she's always criticized for it because she's a girl. You're helping her dream come true, and she's good at it."

"He's right, Hank. I'm stubborn, but I don't think I could have had the courage to take a serious stand for what I want out of life if not for you."

Abraham's voice trembled as he spoke. "You gave me hope. You see me as a person, not as a *colored* person. That means a lot to me. Not only that, you helped me find a home, and you make me feel like I'm family. That's special; *you're* special. You see the world so differently from others because your values are strong, and you aren't afraid to make them known. That's rare, my friend. I don't know about these two, but as far as I'm concerned, I owe you my life because you gave me a chance when no one else would have."

Hank wiped his face with his shirttail. "I don't want any of you getting hurt because of me, but I can't make you back off. I will ask you to please be careful, though. I don't know what else to say except…I'm glad you're my friends. The only thing left to do now, as far as I'm concerned, is tell Mr. Pete what we know and what we suspect. I'll be talking with him tonight. Hopefully, he and the sheriff will have enough to end this."

Beth Ann slapped her knees with both hands. "Well boys, I don't want you to think I'm running out on you, but I promised my dad I wouldn't be too long. He's been really busy today at the clinic. It's been one of those Mondays, and I don't want to add to his worries. Besides, I have homework to do."

"Yeah, me, too. Let us know if there's anything we can do, Hank. I guess you won't be at school tomorrow, either?"

"No, Mr. Pete wants me to stay close till he's sure I'm not in danger from this situation anymore."

"Well, I'll bring you the work assignments if you want. Then you won't be so far behind when you get back."

"I know Ma will appreciate that. I'm just not sure how much I'll be able to do. My concentration lately is about useless. Thanks for coming over this afternoon. I really needed this. I don't know what to think about the stuff you all said about me, but I definitely appreciate your support. It feels good to know I'm not in this alone." Hank sighed. "I'm supposed to go to Granny's with Abraham after I get my chores done. So I guess I'd better get to them."

Abraham stood before anyone else and reached out a hand, helping Beth Ann up first and then Daniel and Hank. "Come on, now. Let's let these two go on before they get into trouble. I'll help you with your chores, and then we can go on over to Granny's. She's expecting us to be on time for supper."

* * * * * * *

The sun was getting low on the horizon when the chores were finished on the Baker farm, but there was still at least thirty minutes of light left— enough time to help Abraham with his chores. They took the shortcut Hank had used when he worked for Granny in July.

As they neared the clearing at the back of Granny's property, Hank searched the woods where he'd buried the bootleg whiskey. He knew the general area where it was located, but he was satisfied he still couldn't tell exactly where he had dug the hole. He hoped no one else would be able to find it, either. He absently rubbed the back of his neck as a familiar feeling of foreboding crept into his thoughts. *Oh, no.* All of a sudden, he sensed an alarm he couldn't shake.

Just before they exited the woods, Hank heard a thud a few hundred yards to his left. He stopped and whispered. "Hold up. Did you hear that?"

Abraham stepped alongside Hank, his eyes wide open. "Not sure. What did *you* hear?"

Hank stood still and quiet for several seconds, listening and searching for the source of the noise. "I think we're being watched— maybe followed."

"Do you see anyone?"

"No, but that doesn't mean there's no one there."

Hank looked deep into the brush, past trees already losing their leaves as cooler weather settled over the region. He thought he saw movement between two large pine trees, but he couldn't be sure. "Let's get out of here. I'll feel better when we're clear of these woods."

"You don't have to tell me twice. Just make sure you let Deputy Collins know about this, too. Don't leave anything out. Your life may depend on it."

"Like you said, you don't have to tell me twice. He's going to know it all. Now, let's get out of here so we can get your chores done before dark."

* * * * * * *

Hank knew the drive from Granny's to the Baker home was short, but he was afraid he'd lose his nerve if he waited to speak with Mr. Pete. His nerves were rattled so much his knees, elbows, and hands shook. As soon as they got in the motor car, Hank told Mr. Pete everything: His suspicions concerning Mr. Morgan and his possible link to the escaped prisoners, the mystery of his missing hat and finding it on his bed, how he got the scrapes on his face, both notes, the checkers, the key, the cut rope, and the noise he heard in the woods.

Afterwards, he had difficulty taking a deep breath while he waited for the deputy to say something. Hank looked from Mr. Pete's face to the man's hands on the steering wheel and back to his face several times before the man finally spoke. It seemed to take him several minutes to respond.

Come on, say something, please.

"Is that all this time? You didn't forget anything, did you?"

"No, sir, that's everything. I'm sorry I didn't tell you earlier."

"Why *didn't* you tell me before now?"

"Well…I…I really don't know. I guess I thought it wasn't important."

"How could you think that, Hank? Don't get me wrong. I'm glad you told me about seeing your Uncle Will in town Saturday, but to think what you just told me wasn't important? Son, my heart is in my throat right now when I put what you just told me with what Stan and I learned today. I didn't say anything to you because I don't want to scare you unnecessarily. But what you shared with me is *absolutely* important. It answers pertinent questions and raises others to guide our investigation into all that's connected with the prison break. As I told you this morning, there is *definitely* more going on than we thought at first. The *danger* to your life is *very* real."

Hank's whole body trembled from the cold reality of what Mr. Pete disclosed. "I know."

"Do you?" The deputy closed his eyes as he rubbed his forehead. "I thought you trusted me."

"I *do* trust you. If I didn't, I wouldn't have told you anything."

"Well, something's obviously wrong for you to keep these things from me for so long. Communication is the most important element of any relationship. I'd like to think you would've kept this information from your father, too, if he were still alive, but…"

"Mr. Pete, I never meant to hurt you or our relationship."

The deputy waited several seconds before he reached across the seat and ruffled Hank's hair. "I know. But will you answer my question? Would you have kept this from your dad?"

Hank thought before he answered. "I think so."

"You don't sound very convincing."

"I don't know how to explain it, but…well." Hank sighed. "When Daddy was missing, I talked with him in my thoughts all the time. It was like we were connected somehow. That's why I wouldn't give up on his coming home. Whenever I needed help with something, I'd talk to him as if he were here with me. I could tell him just about everything on my mind. But there were times I was embarrassed to tell him what I was thinking. That's when

I'd hear him tell me I had to figure some things out for myself. Then he'd remind me to act according to how I was taught so my character wasn't in question. I didn't always understand what that meant until you came along.

"You're so much like him, it scares me sometimes. I've told you that before, and it's *still* true. I need to be able to see you for who *you* are and not him. I'm beginning to do that, but this is different. When I talk with you, I have to know who I'm talking to. Is it Deputy Collins or Mr. Pete or...my dad?"

The deputy remained silent for almost a minute. "I hope my job never interferes with our ability to communicate, son. And I understand you have a lot to work through emotionally with my becoming part of the family soon. What I told you when we first met about not being a replacement for your father is just as true today. I love you. That won't change, whether you return that love or not. What matters most to me is that you trust me enough to tell me when something or someone is threatening your life or our family's lives. If something ever happened to you, it would be just like losing my own flesh-and-blood son all over again. You've become that important to me. Please come to me when you have information that is relevant to your safety, no matter how you interpret it. I can't protect my family if you keep facts of this caliber from me."

"I understand. I'll do my best to not disappoint you again."

"Son, I'm not as disappointed as I am frightened that something could have happened to you. It would be very difficult for me to forgive myself if I couldn't protect you properly. If I don't have your complete trust, I can't keep you safe."

"Yes, sir."

Mr. Pete closed his eyes as he pinched the bridge of his nose and yawned. "I don't know about you, but I'm tired. How about we go inside and get some sleep."

"Yes, sir."

When they got out of the motor car, Hank felt the hair on the back of his neck stiffen. The closer they got to the front porch, the stronger the sense of danger became. He stopped and pulled on the deputy's arm. "Mr. Pete?"

The man gently broke contact with Hank's hold. "What are you doing?" Then they made eye contact, and he stopped. "What's wrong?"

"I don't know for sure, but something's not right."

"What are you talking about? Come on, let's go inside."

In just a couple of steps, Hank noticed the front door stood wide open. He stopped again. "Mr. Pete, the front door is open."

The deputy crouched with his hand on his gun without drawing it. "Did you leave it open?"

He slowly shook his head. "No, sir."

"Okay, stand back, away from the house." The deputy drew his gun slowly from his holster and cocked the hammer. He quietly climbed the steps and tiptoed to the door before carefully opening the screen and entering the house.

Chapter 20

Hank stepped several feet into the yard, away from the porch steps. He cringed as the hinges on the screen door creaked. The sound seemed to reverberate off the tree line at the edge of the woods surrounding the farm. When something fell inside the house the moment the deputy entered, Hank instinctively crouched where he waited. He forced himself to stay put.

"Mr. Pete!"

Within a few seconds, the deputy showed himself at the doorway. "It's all right, Hank. A chair fell over when I opened the door. That's all."

"Can I come in?"

"No. Stay where you are. I want to check the rest of the house first."

It seemed to take hours for Deputy Collins to reappear. Hank noticed he no longer carried his gun in his hand. When the deputy joined Hank in the yard, his lips were pursed in a scowl.

"Someone's been here while we were at Granny's. They trashed the house. I'm glad your ma isn't here to see it." Mr. Pete looked back at the dark house, his arms akimbo. "I know you're tired, son. So am I, but this can't wait. I need you to start in your room and check everything. Make sure to make a list of anything missing. If you find something that doesn't belong here, don't move it. Call out and I'll come to you, so I can see it where it was left. Do you understand?"

"Yes, sir."

"Good. When you finish with your room, move on to your ma's bedroom. I'll check her sewing room and the parlor. We'll both check the kitchen."

"Yes, sir."

"Hank, it's a mess in there, so be prepared. I need to document what we find for the official police report. Try to leave your emotions out here. There'll be time to be angry later. Right now, we have a job to do. Don't worry about cleaning anything up tonight. We'll come back and do that long before your ma comes home."

"Yes, sir. You're not going to tell her? But won't she…"

"Yes, son, I'm going to tell her. We don't keep things from one another. That's what good communication is all about. I'm just glad she doesn't have to deal with this *and* Jimmy's recovery while her emotions are so stretched. But given the nature of mothers and my experience with Granny Rose, I'd be willing to bet she already senses something else has happened. So keeping it from her would be foolish." They smiled. "All right, let's get to work."

* * * * * * *

Getting through the house was tricky at best. Broken glass, books, and various items were thrown helter-skelter in the parlor. *Whoever broke in was looking for something specific.* Hank's heart shattered when he saw his daddy's military display case smashed. It lay mangled in a heap with the flag from his casket, pictures, ribbons, and medals scattered not far from it. He ground his teeth together, and his nostrils flared as rage boiled in his gut.

Remember what Mr. Pete said. "Try to leave your emotions out here. There'll be time to be angry later. Right now, we have a job to do." I'll try to keep calm for now, but I'd love to smash the guy's face that did this.

He forced his feet to move on to the hallway as his fingernails bit into his flesh from his clinched fists. Each step resounded with the crunch of what was left of precious memorabilia. Once again, the realization he was somehow the target of this mess stirred the embers of guilt he had tried to extinguish. *If I had just told Mr. Pete everything before now, this might not have happened. How do I explain that to Ma?*

When he saw his room, sorrow overwhelmed him as tears flowed down his face. The beds were stripped of linens, and the mattresses were on the floor. He was both glad and surprised they hadn't been slashed. The picture frame with his daddy's silver star in it was broken, and the medal was gone. He felt pinpricks along his hairline. He no longer fully contained his anger. *No! Not the medal!* Heat radiated from his face and neck. He frantically looked through the clothes, books, and trinkets scattered all over the floor, and then he searched the emptied drawers for the relic.

His eyes stung as he stood in the middle of the room and made himself dizzy, trying to decide where to search next. When his gaze stopped momentarily on his bed, his mind flashed on the memory of finding his hat there. *Check the closet.* The shelf had been swept of everything, but he looked there anyway. Then he tossed through his clothes and shoes without finding the medal.

As he turned his attention back to the room, he felt drawn to the pillows. He stepped over heaps of linens and clothes to get to them at the foot of his bed. With shaking hands, he picked up first one pillow, then the other. Under the second pillow was a folded piece of paper. *Oh, no! Another one?* He reached to pick it up with trembling hands, and then froze in place. He remembered Mr. Pete's instructions. *"If you find something that doesn't belong here, don't move it. Call out to me so I can see it where it was left"*

Hank returned to an upright position, eager and reluctant to read the note. "Mr. Pete, I found something."

Within a few seconds, Deputy Collins stepped under the lintel of the boys' bedroom door, his hands braced on the doorjambs. "What is it?"

Hank still held the pillows while he turned his head to look at the deputy. "I think it's another note. I found it under my pillows."

"Did you read it?"

"No, sir, I did as you asked."

* * * * * * *

As soon as Hank saw the note, he knew who had his daddy's medal. *Uncle Will, why are you doing this?* He listened as Mr. Pete read out loud:

WE TOLD YOU WE KNEW HOW TO GET TO YOU. NOW, WHERE'S THE KEY? WHEN WE GET IT BACK, YOU'LL GET YOUR MEDAL BACK. WE HAVE NO INTENTIONS OF DOING ANYTHING TO IT. WE JUST WANT WHAT'S OURS AND KNEW YOU'D UNDERSTAND THE IMPORTANCE OF RETURNING IT. YOU KNOW WHERE TO LEAVE IT. YOU HAVE TILL NOON TOMORROW. THERE WON'T BE A THIRD CHANCE TO SET THIS RIGHT.

"Do you still have the other notes you told me about?"

"Yes, sir." He pulled them from his trousers pocket and gave them to Mr. Pete.

"The penmanship's the same. Tell me again, why do you think these are from your Uncle Will?"

"He told me I caused problems for him and his cohorts, just like my daddy did. Read the first note. See the connection? What would *you* think?"

The deputy read the first note and nodded. "I see what you mean. You're making a logical assumption, all right."

"Why is he doing this, Mr. Pete? Family isn't supposed to do this to their kin."

"I don't know, son. Sometimes, family relationships are complicated. I'm sorry he turned out this way." He read all three notes again, silently, and then shook his head. "I have my own question for him. What's so important about that key? You said you hid it. Where? I'd like to see it."

Hank reached under his shirt and pulled out a makeshift necklace made from a long strand of yarn from Ma's sewing basket. The key dangled from it. "It's right here." He passed it over his head and put it in the deputy's outstretched hand.

Deputy Collins examined it for several seconds. "It looks like it goes to a strongbox."

"That's what I thought."

Mr. Pete stepped over the mess on the floor to the window, his back to the room, as he tapped the key against his open palm. When he turned back around, Hank saw a slow grin spread across the man's face.

"Now that we know what he's after, I say we give it to him."

Hank's heart leapt with hope for the first time in days.

Then, for an instant, the deputy's grin faltered. "No…"

Disquiet crept into Hank's thoughts as he registered Mr. Pete's hesitation. He looked away, his hope all but crushed. "What?"

The deputy put his hands on Hank's shoulders. "Hang on. Don't sound so glum. I think I have a better idea. Hear me out." He waited for Hank to look him in the eyes, and then he smiled. "I think I know how to get to the bottom of this, maybe everything. How would you like to catch this guy as my partner, a junior deputy? Of course, I need to clear it with Stan in the morning, but with careful planning, we could sell him on the idea and very likely end this shortly after noon tomorrow."

Hank's hope revived with cautious optimism. "You mean it?"

Mr. Pete's smile widened as he nodded. "Yes, I do." He then stood tall and offered Hank his outstretched hand. "We'll do it together. You deserve to know the truth from the source. We both do. What do you say…partner?"

* * * * * * *

Sunlight streamed through the boards forming the walls of the hayloft, waking Hank from a restful, dreamless sleep. He was surprised he had slept at all. When they had finished taking stock of the damage done to the house, Mr. Pete suggested they bunk in the hayloft since it was too late to go to Granny's. Hank sat up, yawned, and stretched, all at the same time, and then he looked over where the deputy had bedded down. His bedding was already neatly rolled and set against the wall under one of the closed windows in the loft, but Mr. Pete was nowhere in sight.

Hank got up and dressed quickly in the crisp, morning air. As he rolled his own bed, he heard the barn door open and shut. He stopped what he was doing and sneaked to the ladder, holding his breath, and peaked over the edge. When he saw the deputy cross the space between the door and the ladder with what looked like a pan covered with one of Ma's dish towels, he let out a sigh of relief.

"You made us something to eat?"

The deputy stopped in his tracks and looked up at Hank, his smile heartwarming. "Hey, good, you're awake. Yeah, do you find that so hard to believe?"

"Well, yeah…no…I mean…"

Mr. Pete chuckled. "I learned from the best."

"Granny Rose?"

"Yep. She wanted to know I could take care of myself when I moved out on my own after Rachel died. So she made me learn how to cook, clean, do my own laundry. She was brutal."

They both chuckled then.

"You are hungry, I hope."

"Yes, sir. I think my growling stomach is what woke me up."

"Really?"

Hank chuckled again. "No, not really."

"Ah, humor. That's different from your behavior of late. It's a good sign."

"Yeah, it's amazing what happens to a body when you come clean with things. I guess it's true what they say."

"What's that?"

"Confession's good for the soul. But I'd say it's good for the body, too."

"Well, if you want to know the truth, you can't have one without the other."

"Not if you listen to Daniel."

"Huh?"

"Ghosts?"

"Oh. Well, let's eat."

They sat with their legs dangling off the edge of the loft eating hot biscuits and freshly churned butter from the icebox.

"By the way, I'll be going to the icehouse before coming home today. So what do you think? I know they're not your ma's biscuits."

"They're all right, Mr. Pete. But don't quit the job you already have. I'm afraid you won't be hired for this one. We have an expert cook living here who won't give it up that easily. Besides, you forgot the honey."

"You think you're funny, don't you?"

"Hey, you asked."

"It's good to have you back, son. I've missed you."

"It feels good to not be afraid. I'm a little nervous about the plan, though. I don't want to mess up, but I'm not afraid. I know you'll have my back, and I'll have yours. You can count on me."

"It's okay to be a little afraid. It keeps us careful. We just have to make sure it doesn't become so exaggerated it robs us of being sensible. Fear can be useful as long as it doesn't take charge."

"Yes, sir."

"Now, will you be all right doing your chores alone so I can go to the office and fill Stan in on our plan?"

"Yes, sir."

"Good. It shouldn't take long, but don't worry if it takes a couple of hours. I want to make sure we have proper back-up should something happen we didn't foresee. When I get back, we'll put things in motion. So be ready."

"Yes, sir."

* * * * * *

As Hank did his chores, he thought about the break-in and Uncle Will's obvious involvement. In some ways, the destruction reminded him of stories aunts and uncles and cousins told at the family reunion last October out at Grandpa Calvin's near Hampton. They described the aftermath of a tornado that had ripped through some of their homes that spring. The similarity helped keep Hank's emotions in check. It happened; it's over. What's left is restoration.

I'm glad Mr. Pete's here, Daddy. I hope you'll understand when I call him "Dad" that I'm not setting you aside. Would it be all right if I make him your partner?

When he returned to the yard from putting the basket of eggs on the kitchen counter and walked toward the barn, Hank felt the familiar need to rub the nape of his neck.

Use fear, don't let it use you. Keep your wits, Hank.

He stopped in his tracks about halfway from the house to the barn and turned in a complete circle, slowly looking for anything out of the ordinary.

Trust your heart and not your eyes, Hank. Act wisely because there will be times you'll need to trust your eyes and not your heart.

"Not again…wait…Daddy? Is that you? Are you telling me something?" At the same time he saw the smoke billowing from the hay loft windows, he smelled it. "Oh, no! The barn…the animals…"

Panic prevented Hank's feet from moving. "Oh, God…I need your help. Show me what to do."

Immediately, his mind and body worked together without hesitation.

Get the animals out first.

Hank ran to the barn and swung open the doors, securing them so the livestock could make a run for their lives. He went to each stall and opened the gates, slapping the animals' rumps and shooing them out. His eyes stung and his cough became congested the longer he stayed in the barn. Just as he freed the last of the cows, he felt a heavy blow on the back of his head. Everything went black immediately.

Chapter 21

Hank was wet with sweat when the fog of unconsciousness lifted. His chest cavity burned as his body convulsed from painful coughs. He tried to quiet them when he heard someone shout his name from far away. He opened his eyes and sat up. The back of his head hurt, but not as severely as the last time he was hit. He winced when he touched the goose-egg-sized bump.

Thick smoke filled the small room as he took in his surroundings. *Where am I?* Then he remembered what he'd been doing just before he was ambushed. That's when he noticed the harnesses. Suddenly, the cloud of confusion cleared completely.

I'm right under the loft in the tack room. It's on fire. I've got to get out of here.

He tested the door for heat, and then he pushed on it. It wouldn't budge. *There must be something blocking it.* Then he heard his name called from inside the barn. It didn't sound like Mr. Pete, but the voice was familiar.

"Help, I'm in the tack room! Help!" He pounded on the door, unconcerned about the splinters piercing his skin. His coughing doubled him over.

The next time he heard his name, it was muffled; but the voice was close.

His own voice was weak. Every time he breathed in, he coughed. "I'm in the tack room."

"Hang on. I'm here. The door's jammed."

Another coughing fit wracked Hank's body. He was losing consciousness without the ability to breathe fresh air. His insides burned and sweat soaked his clothes. He lay on the floor in a fetal position. Just as he closed his eyes, he felt someone lift him and carry him out of the room. When he was deposited gently on the soft, cold ground, he opened his eyes and saw the back of the head of his rescuer. He deduced the man was listening for his heartbeat. Breathing was labored at best, but he was alive.

Hank's voice was raspy. "Thank you for saving me." When the man sat up and looked at him, Hank gasped. "Mr. Morgan?"

"My young friend, I'm so glad I got here in time. But when I saw the flames, I thought I was too late." Tears streamed down the giant's face. He looked back at the structure as it collapsed into a heap of burning rubble. "I just wish I'd gotten here in time to save the barn, too."

Hank sat up and swallowed the vomit rising in his throat as he considered the full impact of what had happened. *What if...no, stop it! Don't think about the "what if's." You're safe. That's what matters most.*

"Don't worry, Mr. Morgan. It's not your fault. How'd you know I was in there?" Hank dismissed his earlier suspicions of the man as he reminded himself not to judge him without proof. He realized he was happier than ever to see his friend had returned.

"How else would the animals have gotten out?" The giant's lopsided smile matched the friendliness of his dark brown eyes. "Besides that, Pete told me where you were and asked me to wait here for him with you. He said he had a couple more things to do before he had everything ready. Then he'd join us. He told me about the break-in and the plan."

"You're part of our plan? I don't understand."

The big man's eyes twinkled and a grin spread across his face. "You will, just be patient. Pete's in charge of this operation, so he should be the one to tell you. Besides, it'll take more time to explain than we have right now. We need to dig a trench around the barn so the fire doesn't spread to the house."

* * * * * * *

When Mr. Pete finally showed up, the trench was about half finished. Hank watched the deputy take control of his emotions as his pale, worried face became red with rage. Hank was impressed with how the deputy used the intensity of his anger to spur himself into action. He helped dig the rest of the trench to save their farm from utter destruction. With the three of them working together, the task was completed, to the satisfaction of the men, with almost fifty minutes to spare before the noon deadline.

Hank was concerned Mr. Pete would leave him behind once Mr. Morgan told him what happened when he arrived.

"Are you sure you want to go through with this, son?"

"Yes, sir, I'm ready." *Follow his example.* "I'm not afraid anymore; I'm mad."

"Whoa, now, check those emotions and leave them here. Just like last night, we have a job to do. There'll be time to deal with your anger later. Until then, I need you to be focused on your part of this gig."

"Yes, sir, I know. I understand." Hank grinned, feeling good about what they were about to do. "Gig?"

Mr. Pete's smile encouraged Hank all the more. "Yep, gig. This is one of the reasons I joined the force, to catch criminal idiots when they're at their stupidest." He checked his pistol and nodded toward Mr. Morgan as he holstered it again. "Okay, boys, it's time. We need to go. Don't worry, son, if you don't see us. We don't want to spook this guy."

"Yes, sir. Did you just call Uncle Will a criminal idiot?"

"You'll see what I mean. Do you have the key?"

Hank patted his stomach. "Right here under my shirt, hanging around my neck."

"Good. Let's do this."

* * * * * * *

The trek through the woods to the fishing hole took about ten minutes. As soon as they were under the canopy, Mr. Pete and Mr. Morgan left Hank to go on alone. He never heard the men move about the forest.

I wonder if Mr. Pete will teach me how to do that. Not now, Hank. Concentrate on the task at hand. I hope my voice doesn't crack. God, help me stay strong and not show fear. He was surprised he had prayed when he normally talked to his daddy instead.

As he neared the place he and his friends called Catfish Haven, he slowed his steps, looking for any sign of his companions as well as Uncle Will. *I'll be able to see better when I climb the rock.* He jogged the rest of the way to the site and stopped at the base of the flat-topped rock. When he looked up, the sun was directly overhead from what he could see of it through the treetops.

"Good, you're on time."

The voice came from above. Hank watched Uncle Will lean out over the edge of the rock. Hank scrunched his brows together.

There's still something not quite right about him, but I don't get it. What's different?

"Come on up; it's really nice up here. You can see quite a ways in every direction. But you already know that, don't you?"

"You come down here. After last night and this morning, you don't give me much reason to trust you won't just toss me into the river to the gators or the whirlpools."

"What? Why would I do that? We're family."

"That's funny coming from you, and I don't mean 'ha ha' funny. Family respects their kin. You disrespected Ma, your *sister*, when you almost got her in trouble with the government in June and then again when you destroyed our home last night. As if that weren't enough, you desecrated my daddy's memory and character when you stole his medal. And then you showed your cowardice when you trampled on the flag and his service to the United States of America.

"And that wasn't all. You had to come back this morning and do more damage? In the process, you tried to kill me, to say nothing about nearly killing Jimmy yesterday with the tire swing you had rigged *for me*. You have a twisted idea of what you mean by family."

Uncle Will's haughty expression changed into one of abject fear as his smug smile became a scowl with deep furrows between his brows. "Tire swi…? What are you talking about? I wasn't…"

"Prove it. Come down here and talk to me like a man for a change."

Uncle Will climbed down from the rock without hesitation. When he faced Hank, the man grabbed his upper arms with white-knuckled hands and squeezed. Hank winced. "Tell me exactly what you're talking about. Start with this morning. Whatever happened, it wasn't me."

Before Hank could utter a word, he watched Mr. Pete quietly approach them from the trail behind his captor. His gun was drawn and pointed skyward. Mr. Morgan was still out of sight.

"Go ahead, Hank, and tell our friend here what happened this morning. I believe he's telling the truth."

It was Hank's turn to scowl as Uncle Will gasped and released him. The man spun around and raised his hands. The deputy had a cocked gun aimed at his chest.

"Are you all right, son?"

Hank stepped away from the men, the scowl deepening on his face. *He knows something…* "Yes, sir, but why do you believe him?"

"You see, Hank, this is *not* your Uncle Will. The sheriff went to the penitentiary yesterday and had a long, enlightening visit with your uncle. They had quite a chat."

"What?"

"Let me introduce Detective Sullivan Marshall from the Pinkerton Detective Agency. He's been working in disguise as your uncle all this time in order to get inside a dangerous band of criminals trying to form a syndicate of sorts in the Smackover oil fields. They're trying to corner the market on bootleg whiskey, cotton, lumber, and now oil."

"Is Uncle Will going to be all right?"

"He's recovering nicely, and you'll be happy to know he's a changed man. Really. Oh, and you can put your hands down, detective. But you'll pardon me if I keep my gun handy." Mr. Pete released the hammer and put it back in the holster.

The detective's Adam's apple bobbed several times, his brows furrowed. "Look, I can explain everything."

Hank stepped toward the men as he flexed his fists at his sides. "Where's my daddy's medal?"

"Wait, son. We'll get to that and the other charges against him later. First, I need to hear what he knows about the fire and the assault on you this morning."

"I really don't know anything about a fire. You were assaulted, boy?"

"Yes, sir, I was. Someone knocked me out and locked me in the tack room after setting the hay on fire in our barn. I could have died except Mr. Morgan came along."

"Morgan? Jeffrey Morgan? He's here?"

Just then, Mr. Morgan approached the group from the opposite side of the woods from where Mr. Pete had come. His brows were furrowed deeply over eyes with a fearsome glare at the detective. Hank gasped and watched the detective cower.

"I figured you were the one behind all of this, Marshall."

"Mr. Pete? I'm really confused."

"It's all right, son. Jeffrey, Mr. Morgan, is with the William J. Burns' Bureau of Investigation. He's been on assignment, building a case against Detective Marshall. You see, many of the Pinkerton detectives use unscrupulous methods and tactics to bring in criminals. But unlike most of his co-workers, Mr. Marshall's shameful use of children and his unethical practice of endangering lives unnecessarily have put the entire company at risk. They hired Mr. Burns' agency to verify allegations of his behavior while on the job."

"Wait, I never meant for anyone to get hurt. I did my job. I knew there was bad blood between the people William Stuart worked with and Hank. I used it to bring them out into the open. I had the boy under surveillance the whole time."

Mr. Pete's face and neck reddened instantly. He gritted his teeth as his nostrils flared. "Oh, really, you had him under proper surveillance while his life was in jeopardy as the barn burned to the ground this morning?" He rushed the detective and slugged him with a fist charged with an intense anger Hank had witnessed firsthand. The detective flew backwards for several feet and landed on his back with a grunt and a thud, but conscious. He rubbed his jaw as he sat up, wiping blood from his nose and mouth.

The deputy took deliberate steps to the detective's fallen form before he squatted beside him, his fists still clenched, his knuckles white. "That was for using my son for your personal service without my permission. Consider yourself lucky I don't do it again for putting his life in danger this morning and nearly getting him killed." Mr. Pete looked at Mr. Morgan. His jaw was clinched and his nostrils flared several more times before he finally relaxed and nodded, ever so slightly.

Mr. Morgan stood at the man's feet with his arms crossed over his chest, his own feet shoulder width apart. "You have something that belongs to Hank?"

The detective pulled the medal out of his shirt pocket and gave it to the giant.

"What about the key?"

"What's the key to, Marshall?"

"It's to a strongbox with evidence in it that proves the existence of a growing syndicate and the list of its members."

"Who's the leader?"

"I don't know. I never saw anything in the box while I was embedded with them. I was just the key keeper. When I lost it, they threatened to do to me what they'd done to George Blackman. That's why I did what I did. I was desperate…"

"Mr. Pete, did you hear that?"

"Yeah, I have some questions for him about this information, if you don't mind, Jeffrey."

"Sure, go ahead."

"What do you know about George Blackman, Marshall?"

"He was working on behalf of the Pinkerton Detective Agency. We figured he would be able to get the information we needed to bring the group down. Then we learned he'd been killed. That's why I'm here. My assignment was to finish what he started."

"Did his family know that he was working as a detective?"

"He wasn't. He was an informant. It was to be a one-time operation. He agreed to the mission and the financial arrangement. I don't know if he told his family. We told him the work was dangerous, and we suggested he keep his connection with us to himself."

"What was the arrangement agreed upon?"

"When we got the information we needed, we would pay him $1,000."

"And now?"

"Well, I don't know. I guess it's null and void because he died."

"That would be a big mistake, Marshall. You see, George Blackman's son lives with me and my grandmother. He's one of Hank's best friends. I think the Pinkerton Detective Agency owes *him* that money. I believe his father got the information you needed and died because of it. His family deserves the truth and the money. Abraham can use it to take care of his mama and siblings. Wouldn't you say that was fair, Jeffrey?"

"Sounds reasonable. I'll see *Mister* Marshall speaks with his superiors. I'll oversee the transaction myself before I start my new position with the Bureau."

"Good. I think we're done here. Stan will be glad to put this matter to rest. We'll be handling the investigation of this syndicate from now on with the help of what's inside that strongbox since we have the key. By the way, Marshall, where is the strongbox?"

"As far as I know, it's at the Ouachita County Courthouse. I turned it over to my contact in the district attorney's office after I secretly confiscated it from the lumberyard near Miller's Bluff. At the group's last meeting, they laughed when I told them I saw someone hand it over to a sheriff's deputy from Camden. I got nervous when I learned they had someone working for them inside the courthouse. Then I had to tell them the key was missing."

Mr. Pete took the key from Mr. Morgan and put it in his shirt pocket. "Well, I have custody of the key, now. I'll be taking a trip to the courthouse when we're finished here and will be wrapping up that investigation, too. Jeffrey, you'd better take this guy away. I don't trust myself with him."

The giant chuckled as he handcuffed the former detective. "I understand. I'll see you later. And Hank, we have unfinished business to discuss tonight, okay?"

"Yes, sir."

"Pete, I'd like you to sit down with us, too."

He nodded. "Sure thing. See you tonight at Granny's."

Mr. Pete put his arm around Hank's shoulders as they watched Mr. Morgan and the detective head down the trail toward the Baker property. "Well, how does it feel to know your first *official* case ended successfully, partner?"

He looked up at the deputy. "It feels really good. You said, 'first case.' Does that mean we'll do this again?"

"Maybe, when the time is right, that is."

"Thank you for including me today. But I think I'll leave the detective work to you and Daniel. I'd rather stick with my plans to be a reporter, if you don't mind."

Mr. Pete smiled. "As long as you print the facts responsibly, I don't have a problem with that."

"So now…what will happen to Mr. Marshall?"

"I honestly don't know. I'm just glad you're safe, and he's gone from here."

"Yeah; me, too."

"Let's get you back to Granny's so I can go to Camden before it gets too much later."

"If you don't mind, I think I'd like to start cleaning up the house."

"Are you sure?"

"Yes, sir."

"Okay, but don't forget. I'm taking tomorrow off to help. But honestly, it could take a few days to get it back to your mom's standards."

"I know. I just need to work off some of this adrenaline so I don't go nuts. Then there's the barn."

"Yeah, the barn. How am I going to explain all this to your mom?"

"I'm so glad you talked me into giving the family's responsibility over to you."

"I'll just bet you are. Have I ever told you how impeccable your timing is lately?"

"What does *that* mean?"

Mr. Pete laughed out loud. "I'll explain it to you later, son."

Chapter 22

Emotions ran high in Granny's kitchen and around her table after supper while they waited for Jeffrey to arrive. Hank helped Granny with the dishes as Mr. Pete told Abraham about the circumstances surrounding his daddy's being in Farmville and his death. Tears flowed easily out of grief as well as joy for the bittersweet news. When Abraham learned about the money, he cried harder. It took several minutes before anyone spoke.

"Don't get me wrong, sir. I appreciate you getting the money for us and all because the Lord knows my mammy could use it. But I'm more grateful Pappy died trying to do something good instead of the way so many of our people die."

Mr. Pete took a sip of his coffee and nodded. "I understand, son. You're not the only one in this room who has had to fight for a place in the white man's society. I, for one, definitely respect your attitude. You're a good man, Abraham. You do your family, not just your father, great honor. I think I speak for Granny, Hank, and the others when I say we're better for having you as our friend than if we had missed that opportunity. And I think you know who I mean."

Abraham nodded as he smiled. "Yes, sir, I do."

"Mr. Pete, will those responsible for Mr. Blackman's death be punished?"

"That's for the courts to decide, Hank. We hope so. When I get back from the courthouse tomorrow, we'll start those wheels to moving in that direction."

"As far as I'm concerned, Hank, it really doesn't matter if they do or not."

Hank's brows furrowed. "But why not?"

"Because you have to ask yourself what's more important, getting justice here or grace? My pappy is in heaven with Jesus because he received God's grace while he was here. As far as that's concerned, what those men did to him was done to Jesus, too. He believed that and lived it every day of his life. Besides, what can we do to them that God can't do better when it's all said and done? So what if they get away with it here. Will they get away with it for eternity? No one escapes justice from God forever."

"I don't know. I'll have to think about that a while."

Granny sat down before she joined the conversation. "You do that, Hank. But hear his words carefully. He didn't say we don't have a responsibility to bring criminals to justice when we can. So they haven't gotten away with anything yet."

"That's right, boys. I didn't get all the paperwork finished at the office in time to get to Camden before the courthouse closed for the day, but there's still tomorrow. I plan to be there first thing in the morning with the proper warrants to bring that strongbox back to Farmville. Then Stan and I will open it and begin the official investigation from the evidence inside it. Until then, we'll just have to be patient."

Within a few minutes, the clock on Granny's mantle in the parlor struck eight, and Granny turned in for the night. The deputy stood at the kitchen sink and looked out the window.

Hank joined him, mimicking his stance. "Is something wrong, Mr. Pete? You're fidgeting."

"I'm concerned about Jeffrey. He should have been here by now."

"Did you know Mr. Morgan was an agent with the Burns' Bureau?"

"I knew he was considering it, but I didn't know he had completed the training."

They rejoined Abraham at the table.

"Daniel will be thrilled. He'll probably ask him to get Mr. Burns' autograph for him. He found out a couple of weeks ago that Mr. Burns is called 'America's Sherlock Holmes.' I think he told his parents he wants his books for Christmas." They all smiled. "I'm glad I was wrong about him...Mr. Morgan, that is."

"Sometimes, we just have to trust our instincts about people and not let anything other than facts shatter our faith."

Hank gasped as he thought about the words the voice inside his head repeated over the past few days. *"Trust your heart and not your eyes, Hank. Act wisely because there will be times you'll need to trust your eyes and not your heart."* All of a sudden, his pulse raced through his veins. "That's it! That's what it means?"

Mr. Pete and Abraham looked at one another, then Hank, with puzzled expressions.

"The voice from my dream told me to trust my heart and not my eyes." Hank looked at Abraham. "Do you remember me telling you about it?"

"No, you must be thinking of Daniel and Beth Ann."

"Oh, yeah, you're right. Sorry. Anyway..."

"What are you talking about, son? Is this something you forgot to tell me about when you *supposedly* told me everything else?"

"Uh...not really...it wasn't part of everything else. It was from a dream I had. A voice kept telling me the same thing over and over. It said, 'Trust your heart and not your eyes. Act wisely because there will be times you'll need to trust your eyes and not your heart,' or something like that. Your comment about trusting our instincts about people until facts proved otherwise made the voice's words *finally* make sense."

"Uh, okay…"

Just then, the back door opened into the kitchen. Mr. Morgan ducked as he stepped through the doorway, his head just inches from the ceiling when he straightened. His brows were furrowed, and his frown was foreboding.

The deputy stood slowly, his mannerism stoic. "Jeffrey, what took you so long?"

"Pete, boys, I'm sorry, but it couldn't be helped. I just came back from Camden. The news isn't good."

Hank's heart jolted and skipped a couple of beats. "Is it about Mr. Marshall?"

"No, he's all right. But I can't say the same for the courthouse." Immediately, Mr. Pete looked like he was about to pounce. "What about the courthouse?"

"It burned to the ground while we were talking with Marshall here. By the time I got there, it was fully engulfed. I stayed till we searched through everything in the rubble for the strongbox. It's gone."

Mr. Pete slumped back in his chair. "Gone?"

"As hot as the flames were, they're thinking it melted and the contents were destroyed. But there's really no way to know for sure. It's possible someone took it before the fire started."

"Do they know what caused the fire? I mean, is there a logical explanation or a natural cause?"

"It's under investigation, but there's a high chance it was intentionally set. No one was hurt, but all the records, like the building, are a total loss. If what Marshall told us is true, I'm thinking there may have been someone on the local syndicate's payroll working at the courthouse. He could have set it. I'm not sure we'll ever know for sure."

Mr. Pete bowed his head, shaking it until he looked in Abraham's direction. "I'm so sorry, son. I guess we'll never know who killed your father." He pounded his fist on the table, rattling the contents under the cloth Granny used to cover leftovers. "We were so close."

Hank's jaws clenched so tightly his teeth hurt.

"It's not fair. Mr. Pete, Abraham deserves justice. Why is this happening? It's like there's a conspiracy to keep the truth hidden. I mean, I know justice is blind, but these people have justice tied and held captive for their personal gain, too. It's not right."

"No, son, it isn't. That's the rub. There's really nothing we can do."

Abraham laid a hand on the table in front of Hank. "It's all right, Hank. Don't be upset because of what you think is injustice for me and my family. It's not worth the worry."

"But…"

"No." He shook his head. "There are no 'buts.' You remember what I told you about what my ancestors learned from their owner, Mr. White?"

"Yeah, but how does that make this okay."

"It doesn't, but there is more going on here than we can see. Hank, I have to trust my heart, too. And my heart is telling me there's a higher power at work here. My pappy used to tell me to let go of the wrongs done to me because the people doing them don't know any better. They're worldly and acting like their natural selves. He told me to let them be because once they left this world, they would have all of eternity to live in misery. If doing stupid stuff made them happy, it'll be short-lived. Eternity is a lot longer than any lifetime here on earth. So let it go. God is at work here. He will have vengeance on the wrongs we're suffering. It belongs to him, not us."

Mr. Pete cleared his throat as he rubbed his temples, his eyes closed. "Thank you, Abraham." After several silent seconds, he stood, his chair scraping against the floor. He walked around the table to the sink where he gripped the edge of the countertop. No one spoke while he stared out the window for nearly a full minute.

"You know, I joined law enforcement because I believe in the system. I've seen far too much injustice not to enjoy the satisfaction of putting away the bad guys. So when people play the law against their victims, like it was a winning poker hand, and cheat them out of their day in court, my blood boils."

Then he turned from the window and crossed his arms over his chest. The scowl on his face relaxed slowly as he took his seat again. "But you've taught me something tonight, Abraham. Your dad was a very wise man. When people seem to get away with crimes, it's not my personal responsibility to right the wrong, even when it happens to someone I care about. That battle is God's alone. What do you say, Hank? Can we leave it for God to handle in his own way in his own time?"

"Do we have a choice?"

Abraham shook his head. "Not really. At this point, it's a matter of attitude. You have to *decide* whether you're going to give it to him and live peaceably or be miserable while trying to fight a war you won't win."

Mr. Morgan sat down beside Mr. Pete, directly across from Hank. He clasped his hands and set them on the table in front of him. Hank noticed the color of his knuckles alternated between white and red as he squeezed them. "Speaking of war, I need to explain some things that I should have told you when we first met, Hank. But I was afraid."

Hank leaned forward in his chair, his hands clasped between his legs, his knees quaking beneath the table. He leaned his chest against the table edge to keep from being obviously shaky.

Mr. Morgan sighed. "I'm…I'm alive… No, that's not the way to start this. Hank, your daddy died saving my life in France."

Hank felt a numbness begin in his stomach and fan out through his core. "You knew my daddy was dead, but you didn't say anything?"

"No." He shook his head, his eyes teary. "I didn't know he had died until Granny told me not long after I got here." Sobs wracked his body for several minutes.

Mr. Pete put a hand on the giant's shoulder. "Why don't you start at the beginning and take your time."

He nodded. "We were in boot camp together. He befriended me and helped me get through it. I was scared because I wasn't there for the same reason your dad was. A judge had given me a choice: Join the Army or go to jail. But it wasn't much of a choice because I didn't do what I'd been accused of doing. You see, I was always ridiculed as a child and called a coward because I would back down from a fight. But I was afraid to fight because of my size. The kids gave me a nickname: the Cherokee word for 'coward.' Don't worry about what it was. You couldn't pronounce it anyway. When my father and brothers took to calling me the same name, I withdrew from everyone and became a loner.

"Then one night, a man I grew up with tried to get me to fight him in a bar, but I ignored him. He responded by breaking a bottle over my head. I grabbed his arms and picked him up off the floor, but that's all I did. When I came to my senses, I put him down and left. That was the last time I ever took a drink of alcohol or went to a bar.

"The next morning, the local lawman on the reservation arrested me for attempted murder. If the man hadn't regained consciousness, I would have probably gone to prison for life. Instead, he woke up and cleared me. But the judge was concerned my frame of mind at the time was to seriously injure him when I picked him up. It didn't matter that I hadn't actually done anything to him. So he charged me with assault with intent to do bodily harm and gave me the choice of the Army or six months in jail. So I joined the Army.

"If it hadn't been for your father, Hank, I don't know if I would have made it. He didn't know my story, but he didn't care. He became my best friend. I was glad we were part of the same unit when we were shipped overseas. The other guys in our company called us twins. We were always together— brothers who took care of one another. And we did so through every battle until that one at Belleau Wood.

"I'll just tell you the fighting was very intense. You don't really need to know the details. We lost a lot of men over the course of that long engagement. The longer it lasted the more scared I got. Charles had to talk me through so many bad situations. We both should have died, but he made me feel invincible. He was so strong and brave. I admired him and envied him at the same time, but I never let that cloud our friendship or color our brotherhood.

"On the day I now assume he died, we were helping a family get out of the line of fire. It was his idea to draw straws to see who would get the family to safety and who would hold off the troops marching straight for the house. He lost. While I was making sure the family was loaded up on their wagon and on the road away from the battle, he was holed up in the barn, firing at the enemy, making himself a target instead of us.

"Once I knew the family was safe, I ran back to the farm and watched him take aim right before a grenade went through the window where he stood and blew up. When I called out his name, they turned their weapons on me. That's the last thing I remember before I woke up in an Army field hospital a couple of days later. I had taken four bullets and survived.

"When I asked about your dad, no one could tell me anything. They kept telling me he's probably in another hospital somewhere else, but he wasn't. I assumed he'd made it because he always managed to escape the worst attacks up till then. We joked about his nine lives because we both knew he should have died more times than we cared to count.

"You don't know how many times I have wished it had been me who died instead of him. He was a good friend. When I found out where he was from, it just felt right. His family lived here, and so did some of mine."

Hank swallowed back tears. "So you really are related to Granny Rose?"

"Yeah, I am." He smiled. "Pete's my cousin."

Hank looked at Mr. Pete. "Did you know any of this?"

"No, not before now, anyway. We're cousins?"

"Yeah, my grandfather on my mother's side was Aunt Rosie's half-brother."

"This is what you wanted to tell us Friday night?"

"Yeah, but I lost my nerve. After what happened with my father and brothers, I was afraid of what Pete would think of me. I've enjoyed being around people who care for me too much, I guess. I didn't want to risk losing the relationships I had carefully molded."

Abraham sniffed. "I know what you mean. I don't want to lose the friends and family I have here, either. There are no more precious and priceless blessings than friends and family. That's what Mr. White encouraged us to use as our reason for treating people with respect, whether they deserved it or not. He said, 'You never know who will be your friend until you treat them like family.'"

Mr. Morgan's lips trembled as he grinned. "That's what Charles Baker became to me. He was my friend, but he was also my family. I'm so sorry I couldn't save him, but after our first close call with death, I promised him I'd watch after his family if he didn't make it home and I did. That's what I've tried to do since coming here. Now that Pete's marrying Miss Martha, I feel like I can turn that responsibility over to him and know he'll cherish it as much as I do."

Mr. Pete nodded. "I will definitely do that, Jeffrey. You can count on me, but we don't want you to think you're no longer wanted, either."

"Between you and Charles, I've found my place in society. I start training to become an expert within the National Bureau of Fingerprint Investigations next week. You know how much I hate guns. I think I'll better serve society in the fingerprint division of the Bureau than anywhere else."

"I want you to know you'll always have a place here with Martha, me, and the boys when you're in town. I'm sure Granny feels the same way."

"Thank you, Pete. But Hank, you're the one I worry about the most right now. I'm sorry things happened like they did with your father. I hope you'll forgive me for waiting so long to talk with you, especially knowing how difficult his death has been on you. I wish your mom were here, too, but I believe, like Abraham said, there's something bigger and more powerful at work here."

Hank pondered all he had heard for several minutes. He noticed everyone remained quiet and kept a vigil on him as he processed the information. *Trust your heart, son.* Without hesitation, he stood and raced around the table to the giant. He wrapped his arms around his neck in a tight hug that would have crushed a smaller person. Sobs shook his body. He remained there for several more minutes.

When Hank felt strong enough, he stepped back from the man and stood at attention as he saluted the one whom his daddy found worthy of friendship. He kept steady eye contact with the giant as the man stood and returned his salute. Then he turned to leave the kitchen, but the voice offered one more piece of advice before he ran for the solitude of the bedroom. *Act wisely, Hank.* He stopped at the doorway and waited a few seconds. Then he spoke from his heart.

"Thank you, Mr. Morgan, for being my daddy's friend." He paused for several more seconds. "I'm honored to call you my friend, too. Please be careful while you're away, and come back to us as soon as you can."